"Are you telling me I can take you to bed, but not put a ring on your finger?"

Alice grimaced. It sounded pretty blunt when he put it like that. "I don't know why I..."

"Want me to touch you? Need to put your hands on me?" Gabe finished for her.

Heat flooded her upturned face. "Physically I'm a pushover. But that's as far as it goes. The physical stuff passes," Alice informed Gabe pragmatically. "You don't go around marrying someone just because you want..."

"To rip their clothes off? I think the time for talking is gone. Take me to bed, Alice."

Passion™

Kim Lawrence

THE MISTRESS SCANDAL

Passion™

TORONTO • NEW YORK • LONDON
AMSTERDAM • PARIS • SYDNEY • HAMBURG
STOCKHOLM • ATHENS • TOKYO • MILAN • MADRID
PRAGUE • WARSAW • BUDAPEST • AUCKLAND

ISBN 0-373-12256-X

THE MISTRESS SCANDAL

First North American Publication 2002.

This edition published by arrangement with Harlequin Books S.A.

Visit us at www.eHarlequin.com

Printed in U.S.A.

CHAPTER ONE

'GO ON, spit it out.'

'What?' Greg produced an expression of injured innocence from habit rather than a belief it would have any effect on his half-brother, who had an unnerving ability to read him like a book.

He knew too that the languid air—half-closed eyes, long legs crossed at the ankle thrust out before him as he slumped in a deeply padded leather chair—was a blind. Those penetrating dark eyes lightened by disturbing amber flecks were shrewdly, probably cynically, analysing his every gesture. With a rush of honesty he grudgingly conceded that the cynicism was possibly justified; he might have let Gabe down a *few* times in the past—but that was a long time ago…

'The recruitment's going really well. I thought you'd be pleased.'

'I am. We're ahead of schedule. But let's put your brilliance at public relations to one side for the moment, Greg. Spare me the injured dignity and tell me why you've developed a nervous tic.'

'What?' Scanning his handsome face anxiously in a conveniently placed mirror, Greg caught the reflection of his half-brother's sardonic smile. 'Very funny.' With a deep sigh he dropped down into a chair. 'There's this girl.'

'You're amazingly predictable, Greg.' Gabriel MacAllister saw his brother flush and softened the cutting edge of his tone. 'I hope you haven't done anything too stupid. The last thing we want is to upset the natives. You know how much knee-jerk opposition there was to the planning permission originally.'

Stupid...? He had no doubt on a scale of one to ten which number Gabe would select. Anyone but Gabe might have softened up a bit if he'd mentioned how desperately in love he was, but he knew better than to appeal to his brother's softer side—Gabriel MacAllister was as hard as tungsten steel, and right now he was waiting for a reply.

'She's pregnant.' He waited, a sulkily defiant expression momentarily spoiling his open-faced good looks, for his brother's response. 'Well, say something!' he burst out, when all Gabe did was rub the toe of his shinily polished shoe in a thoughtful circle on the carpet. 'Call me an idiot—*hell*!'

'I won't waste my breath stating the obvious,' Gabriel responded, in a soft voice his younger brother found infinitely worse than any screaming histrionics. 'You'd better tell me the whole story.'

He listened carefully, repressing his irritation when the younger man lapsed into the rambling sections which miraculously absolved him from all blame, until Greg had finished.

'*Eighteen.* You did say she was *eighteen*?'

'She's very mature.'

It afforded Gabriel small comfort to see his idiot sibling could still blush guiltily.

'Will you come with me when I tell Mum and Dad?' Sophie pleaded, absently eating the peas her sister was shelling. 'You'll be able to calm things down if they start yelling.'

Alice gave a wry snort; she didn't share her sister's confidence. A gap of ten years separated her from Sophie, who was in their parents' eyes perfect in every way. If Sophie hadn't been so genuinely sweet-tempered her indulged upbringing might have turned her into a spoilt brat. But there was nothing brat-like about her sister; she was impulsive, certainly, but that was part of her charm.

'If?' One darkly feathered eyebrow rose to a quizzical angle.

'You're supposed to be making me feel better, Alice.'

The resentful glare was wasted on Alice, who shifted the angle of her garden chair so that she had a better view of her two-year-old son, who was ignoring the numerous brightly coloured toys in the sandpit in favour of his shoes, which he was filling with sand. His golden sun-kissed little face was a serious mask of concentration. She knew she was prejudiced, but Alice didn't think there had ever been a child born as beautiful as Will.

She got up and placed the discarded sunhat back on his head. 'I give up,' she sighed as William removed it equally firmly, giving her a cherubic smile as he did so. Though a remarkably even-tempered child, Will was already displaying a stubborn streak a mile wide.

'I wouldn't worry, Ally, he won't burn. He really is dark. He certainly takes after Oliver, not you.'

Alice twitched the peak of her baseball cap firmly over her lightly freckled nose and remained silent on the subject of her son's complexion. She found herself recalling their honeymoon, when Oliver had ignored her advice and overindulged in the Caribbean sun on the very first day. He'd been literally untouchable for the rest of their stay.

She rejoined her sister. 'I don't think I'll be doing you any favours to raise false hopes. Be realistic, Sophie. There's going to be tears and yelling—and we're talking about the optimistic scenario here.'

She watched her sister's soft lips quiver, and with a sigh she placed a comforting hand on the young woman's shoulder. The most serious trauma in her lovely sister's life so far had been wearing braces; it wasn't what she'd have termed an adequate preparation for her present situation.

'You know how proud they are of you, Soph, their brilliant baby daughter off to Oxford... And you walk in and announce you're going to have a baby. How do you expect them to react? They still fret about you catching a bus alone. Have you thought this thing through?' she asked worriedly.

'Are you saying I should get rid of it?' Sophie pulled away angrily and glared accusingly at her sister. 'How would you have liked it if anyone had suggested you get rid of Will?' She saw her sister flinch. 'You were a single parent too...Oliver was dead—' She broke off and bit her lip. 'I'm sorry, that was...'

'True,' her sister put in levelly. 'Which means I know how hard it is to bring up a child alone. At night when Will has a temperature—which is *probably* a simple cold but might not be—don't you think I long to have someone else there to share...?' Breathing deeply, Alice bit back the emotional words that suddenly threatened to spill out.

Sophie's expression of stunned amazement almost made her smile.

'I thought... You always seem to cope so well, Ally,' she said, staring at her sister wonderingly.

'I cope, but that doesn't mean I don't sometimes wish there was someone else there to share some of the decisions,' Alice admitted truthfully. She didn't want to be responsible for any false notions her sister might have about the difficulties involved in being a single parent. 'And at least Oliver left me reasonably well provided for financially. And I wasn't suggesting anything...that's your decision.'

Sophie looked into her sister's deep blue eyes and saw

sympathy, love and a total lack of judgement. 'I know,' she confessed with a watery grin.

'And will you be bringing up the baby alone...?' Alice fished delicately.

'Oh, Greg wants to make an honest woman of me.'

'Marriage?' Her neutral tone hid her own grave misgivings. Sophie was so young, and marriage was such a drastic step. 'You don't look over the moon,' she observed shrewdly.

'Oh, that wasn't his initial response. Originally he wanted me to...you know.' Two pink spots appeared on her pale cheeks as her eyes slid from Alice's. 'I guess that's why I was bit sensitive,' she confessed huskily. 'He *says* he loves me...'

Alice could hear the obvious doubt in her sister's wobbly tone. 'And do you love him?'

'I thought I did. *I* ended up comforting *him*. I thought he was...I don't know, strong...'

'Slick' was the word that more readily sprang to Alice's mind. But then, she reminded herself, I'm not eighteen any longer, and Sophie isn't the only one to have been won over by Greg's charm offensive.

Even the most stubborn critics of the siting of a software factory on the outskirts of their picturesque market town had been won over by his smooth persuasiveness and carefully stage-managed and conspicuous community involvement.

Alice, on the other hand, had been won over to the scheme by the number of skilled well-paid jobs advertised locally, and the innovative building that would house the high-tech workforce amidst charmingly landscaped grounds.

'He seemed so sure of himself—of everything!' Sophie looked so bewildered that Alice's heart ached. 'Now he's more concerned about what his precious brother will say than how I'm feeling!' Sophie shook her head. 'I must sound really stupid.' She gave a shaky laugh and ran a hand through her smooth shoulder-length blonde hair. 'I suppose I want what you and Oliver had; he was so *perfect*. You were perfect together.'

Sophie saw the naked anguish that flickered across her sister's face and bit the tongue responsible for causing that pain.

'Still, you've got Will, and he looks more like Oliver every day.'

'So everyone keeps saying,' Alice responded, her eyes fixed on her son who was, unless her memory was playing tricks, the spitting image of his father, from his thick dark wavy hair to his gorgeous velvety eyes.

'You will come? For moral support, I mean?'

'Of course I will,' Alice agreed, knowing full well that the task of calming and comforting their distraught, adoring parents over the next few weeks would inevitably fall to her.

The phone call came out of the blue.

'Mrs Lynn?'

There had been a pause where she ought to have identified herself. The caller repeated himself, and this time just a tinge of impatience coloured that deep, vibrant voice.

Alice gave herself a sharp mental shake. The similarity was uncanny, but the phone had a way of distorting voices.

'This is Alice Lynn,' she confirmed, her voice calm, her palms sweaty.

'I'm Gabriel MacAllister…Greg's brother…'

'I know who you are, Mr MacAllister.' What I don't know, she wanted to say, is why you're calling me.

'We should talk.'

'Why?'

There was a pause, as though her blunt response had taken him by surprise. 'Do you think your sister should marry my brother?' He sounded as though he was discussing the price of shares. Alice's every instinct recoiled from such a cold-blooded attitude. It was none of her business, or his, and she should have told him so.

'No.' Alice heard herself reply with gut certainty.

'Interesting.'

In what way? she wondered.

'I'm staying at the Grange.'

The last time she'd been there had been to celebrate their anniversary. Oliver had had too much to drink and he'd confessed…. Alice felt the beginnings of a headache.

'Would you like to meet me here for lunch?'

'I can't…my son…' She knew she sounded vague and wishy-washy, the sort of person who fell in with other people's wishes, and she didn't like it. Her stomach was still churning just because his throaty drawl had triggered a carefully buried memory…

'Fine, I'll come to you.'

'You don't know where I live,' she began as the worrying impression she was being manipulated intensified.

'Oh, but I do, Mrs Lynn.'

The words carried the slight but definite suggestion that that wasn't all he knew about her. Putting the phone down, Alice felt dazed.

All she knew about Gabriel MacAllister—other than the usual success-story stuff everyone knew—was what Sophie had gleaned from Greg, who had, to Alice's mind, an unhealthy reverence bordering on fear for his brother. Put all the information together and the picture which emerged was of a sinister control freak.

Did you give an omnipotent tyrant afternoon tea? she

pondered, able to summon a wry grin. He'd probably turn up his nose at her supermarket teabags.

'And I doubt he's really into Marmite fingers, Will,' she told her son, wiping the sticky black goo off his face and chubby fingers before she lifted him out of his highchair. 'Nap time for you, young man.'

She could hear Will's spasmodic sleepy baby babble through the nursery alarm as she retrieved the scattered toys from the kitchen floor and placed them in a toy box. It was a task she performed numerous times each day, and as her hands went into autopilot her mind raced.

What was Gabriel MacAllister up to? Despite the fact she thought Greg was the last person in the world Sophie should marry, she felt a deep sense of indignation that he possibly shared her view! Was he protecting the MacAllister millions from grasping schoolgirls? she wondered, glancing at her reflection in the mirror as she straightened.

Her face was lightly flushed from a combination of the mild exertion and temper. She looked with lack of interest at her features. It was only on the rarest occasions since Oliver's death and Will's birth that she looked upon herself as a woman—she was just Will's mum these days.

Once she'd thought she was quite attractive, and she'd known that the combination of a slim, curvaceous body and pretty—some said beautiful—features attracted a lot of admiring attention.

She glanced down at the faded tee-shirt and old jeans she wore and decided there was little possibility that her visitor would think she was going out of her way to impress him. Take sex out of your life and it cut down on the complications considerably, she decided approvingly.

If Will hadn't fallen asleep she might have let the doorbell ring, just to emphasise how unimpressed she was by the royal visitation. But she made do with adopting an expression of cool indifference before letting her visitor in.

The world had gone completely mad—or perhaps she had! Fingers pressed to her pounding temples, she shook her head from side to side in denial.

Alice wasn't even aware she'd been walking steadily backwards until her head made jarring contact with the opposite wall. Her knees folded and she found herself sliding down the wall until she was sitting, knees drawn up to her chest, staring upwards dizzily. The doorway was empty; perhaps she'd been hallucinating.

'You're going to pass out if you keep hyperventilating,' a deep voice observed objectively.

Cancel hallucination! He was kneeling right there beside her. God, he even *smelled* the same. Shockingly her stomach muscles spasmed hotly in excitement as she registered the light, expensive cologne with musky male undertones.

'It's my house and I'll faint if I want to,' she snarled.

'And do you?'

Actually, unconsciousness had a lot to recommend it right now!

'I *never* faint,' she told him emphatically.

Although she had once almost lost consciousness from the sheer unadulterated bliss of being made love to. Did he remember...? Her wide eyes collided with his stunningly sensual dark orbs, spectacular eyes that her mother would have coyly termed 'bedroom eyes'... *He did.*

'I suppose it's too late to pretend I've never met you before?' she croaked.

She tried to match her ironic words with a smile, but her facial muscles wouldn't co-operate. The omnipotent tyrant was wearing a beautifully cut lightweight suit; he looked spectacular. She developed a deep interest in his handmade leather shoes. It was the safest place to look until she regained control of herself.

'I've never actually had a woman fall literally at my feet before.' The nostrils of his chiselled nose flared as his dark glance moved slowly over her slim jean-clad figure.

The way Alice recalled it that had been about the *only* thing she'd not done last time. Heat crawled over her skin and her chest felt impossibly tight as she recalled the texture of his dark olive-toned skin slick with sweat.

'I know I look a complete idiot; there's no need to dwell on the subject.' Businesslike, she tucked her jaw-length brown hair behind her ears and, back pressed to the wall, levered herself upright in one supple sinewy motion. 'You took me by surprise,' she added defensively.

Gabriel—how strange after three years to be able to put a name to the face, not to mention the *body*. He automatically extended a steadying hand which she pointedly ignored.

She had thought perhaps delayed shock had exaggerated the memories of that night. No man really had a physical presence that could reach out across a room and turn your stomach inside out. She'd been wrong. It wasn't just that he was physically just about the most impressive male she'd ever seen, it was more than that—*much more*. The 'more' was in the innately elegant way he moved, the dark intelligence lurking in his deepset eyes and the bone-deep aura of confidence.

She'd sometimes wondered what would happen if their paths crossed again. Would he recognise her? Would she wonder what it was about him that had made her behave so crazily? Now there's a prime example of wishful thinking! *Why is this happening to me?*

Superficially he was very like Oliver; that was what had first made her stare that night. But it wasn't the fleeting similarity to her dead husband that had made her carry on…and on…

Oliver had been nearly six-five too, and broad across the shoulders. But the only exercise Oliver had had the time or inclination for in the last few years of his life had been the occasional round of golf. That combined with the fact he had rarely been without a glass in his hand outside working hours had softened and thickened him around the middle.

There was nothing remotely soft about Gabriel MacAllister, then or now! His belly was washboard-flat and his hips were sleekly lean. Alice raised both hands to her cheeks; they felt inordinately hot.

'Did you know?' she asked with terse suspicion.

'Dark, devious plot time?' Gabriel suggested with a raspy scornful laugh that made her flush. 'You mean have I spent the last three years trying to track down the woman who slipped into my bed and slipped out of it just as casually?' A nerve jumped spasmodically in one lean cheek. 'If it hadn't been for the scratches I might even have thought you were a dream.' The erotic, soul-stealing variety.

'I tried to get on with my life…Alice.' His voice was a low, mocking drawl. 'Such a nice, sweet, innocent little name for a nice, sweet, innocent little housewife.' He looked at her bare left hand where it lay curled tightly around her right forearm. 'Still no ring, I see. Tell me, does your husband know about your little escapades?'

The image flashed into her mind of the ugly expression on Oliver's face when she'd flung her ring at him across the candlelit dining room.

'Escapade in the singular.' She hugged her arm even tighter over her breasts but felt no responding surge of security. She'd not noticed that night how uncompromisingly hard his angular jawline was.

Was he asking her to believe that a ring would have protected her from his advances that night? Highly sexed men like Gabriel, used to getting their own way, were not, in her opinion, big respecters of social convention. He'd got what he wanted, so why was he complaining? She'd got something too, to remind her permanently of that night.

Perhaps I ought to have let him think he was one amongst many? Better a trollop than a silly, weak-willed woman…or does a one-night stand qualify a woman for trollop status these days, irrespective of the extenuating circumstances?

'I was the only one?' Gabriel didn't bother to hide his derisive disbelief. 'I'm flattered.'

'Don't be. You were convenient.'

She hadn't intended her crisp words to be interpreted as a blow for liberated womanhood, but from the brief flash of hot anger which briefly illuminated his bronze-flecked eyes he didn't like her response one little bit.

'You're very frank, Alice.'

'Don't call me that…'

'Why not? It's your name.'

'I don't like the way you say it.' It was like a finger skimming the downy surface of her skin, or maybe a tongue. Her thoughts skittered to a dead stop and dark damp patches appeared down her back where her tee-shirt was adhering to her hot sticky skin. Be sensible. Don't think skin, tongues or anything remotely similar around this man.

'Is that why you're shaking? You were shaking the last time…'

'My car had been stranded in a snowdrift for two hours on that occasion,' she reminded him huskily. What's your excuse now, Alice? Unwillingly she met the derision in his dark, compelling gaze. A shiver slid like ice all the way down her shock-stiffened spine—no man had a right to be that good-looking!

The emergency services had taken her and several other unfortunate travellers to a hotel. People forced together by adversity often shared a unique sense of camaraderie which broke down the usual reserves, and that had been the case that night. The plush foyer had been loud with voices of folk sharing stories and whisky, which the hotel bar had been liberally dispensing.

Alice had felt an odd sense of detachment as she'd stood there with an untouched glass in her hand. Nobody there could have been aware that her numbness extended far beyond her icy fingertips. She'd felt as though her soul had been surgically excised—she'd been empty.

Inevitably it would hurt at some point, but she had wanted to delay that inevitable moment for as long as possible. She'd had no idea where she was, and she hadn't been interested enough to ask. She'd just got into her car after the funeral and started to drive. In her right mind she'd have curtailed her journey when the weather had gone from bad to impossible. That evening she'd recklessly driven on, even when the conditions had become a total white-out.

The dark stranger's appraisal had been frankly sensual, even a little contemptuous, but for some reason this hadn't angered or even flustered Alice. The strange sense of recognition, she had told herself later, must have had something to do with the uncanny resemblance. But the closer he'd come the less he'd looked like Oliver, and the stronger the aura of arrogance and power had become.

'You were trapped in the snow…?'

His deep voice held an unusual rasp that sent a sharp electrical jolt all the way down to her toes. She opened her mouth and gave a soundless gasp. How had she *known* he would sound like that?

Alice ignored the opening he'd left for her name. 'Yes.'

'For how long?'

Her slender shoulders lifted in the dark fake-fur-trimmed coat she'd thrown on over her simple black dress. She fingered the single string of pearls around her throat.

'I don't know,' she replied honestly.

'You're not drinking?'

She shook her head and the barrette that secured her long silky brown tresses came adrift. The rich warm cloud reached all the way to her slender waist.

'I am.'

The throaty confession surprised her. He didn't look or sound drunk, she decided, but there was a certain wild, reckless gleam in his eyes. There were other things there too…

Alice's throat felt very dry when she spoke.

'Were you caught in the blizzard too?'

'No, I have a room…'

'They're turning the lounge into a dormitory for us.' Personally she didn't care if she slept on the snooker table.

'British resourcefulness at its most impressive.' The sultry intensity of his dark-eyed regard had not left her face for a second. 'Would you like to share my room?'

Alice couldn't tell from his expression if he really expected her to take his offer seriously.

'Yes.'

If you discounted *please* she'd continued to say *yes* at all the vital moments during the rest of that long night.

Alice dismissed the distracting images from her head by sheer will-power alone. 'I'm in shock,' she said with icy dignity. 'I didn't expect…'

'Your sordid past to knock on the door?' His helpful suggestion earned him a bitter glare. 'Think how I felt! Greg had led me to believe you might be able to fit me in between baking for the church fête and…' He paused with a frown. 'Sorry, my knowledge of wholesome rural activities is a bit sketchy.'

His patronising drawl made Alice grit her teeth.

'And what do I get…?' The mocking smile faded slowly from his face as he looked at her. 'A lot more than I bargained for,' he admitted huskily. 'You were the most uninhibited lover I've ever had.'

His uninhibited lover went scarlet, and a mortified squeak emerged from her throat.

'Don't say things like that to me!' she ordered fiercely.

'Why? Afraid your husband will arrive home unexpectedly? I'd have thought you thrived on the danger.' He looked into her miserable panic-stricken eyes and then looked away, as though what he'd seen there he'd not been expecting. 'Don't panic. I'm not the kiss and tell type.'

Alice tried to retrieve the shattered threads of her dignity. 'I think you've lost track of why you came here.'

'I think I've lost interest,' he replied outrageously.

'My sister's future is not a subject I feel like joking about,' she told him repressively.

'I wasn't joking,' he muttered, following her into the big kitchen with its farmhouse table and obligatory Aga. 'If it's any comfort,' he remarked, picking up a fluffy teddy bear Alice had missed from the floor and twitching a chewed brown ear, 'I've told Greg he's been criminally irresponsible. It's bad enough the girl's only a kid, *but to not take precautions*!' His lips curled scornfully. 'Have I said something funny?' he enquired icily.

'No,' she managed, with only the faintest quiver of hysteria in her voice. Hopefully Gabriel MacAllister would never appreciate the irony of his scathing assessment.

'Is she anything like you?' he suddenly enquired.

'Who?'

'The sister.'

'No, nothing like me at all. Sophie is very clever and sweet.'

'Trusting and a bit dim if she fell for Greg,' he announced with callous objectivity.

Alice inhaled sharply. Even though she suspected he was baiting her she couldn't help responding defensively.

'Do they hand out Oxford scholarships to dimwits?' she enquired acidly. How *dare* he criticise her sister? 'If my sister fell for your slimy brother's dubious charms you can put it down to lack of experience, not her IQ—she is, after all, *eighteen*. You know what I think of a... Heavens, he's nearly my age, for God's sake!' she exclaimed in disgust.

'Surely not *that* old?' he returned, straight-faced. With no make-up and her simply cut hair emphasising the soft contours of her face and long, lovely neck she could have passed for a teenager herself.

'I have to tell you once more I don't find anything humorous in this situation. Also, I've not the faintest idea why you came here. It's nothing to do with us what they decide to do.'

'On the contrary, it's got everything to do with me. My...our mother considers me responsible for everything Greg does.' He was only half joking. Greg had been born with a heart defect, and despite the fact that surgery had corrected the situation years ago protective old habits died hard.

'And you're scared of your mother, I suppose?'

'I've a healthy respect,' he told her drily. 'And I think you underestimate your influence. According to Greg, your sister listens to what you say, and as the lady herself is nowhere to be seen at the moment... This is a situation that needs sorting out sooner rather than later.'

'What exactly do you mean by *sorting out*?' she asked distrustfully.

Gabriel's expression made it clear he understood the nature of her suspicions. 'Not what you think.' His wry tone made Alice flush.

'I think you misunderstand my relationship with my sister, Mr MacAllister… Granted, we're close, but that doesn't mean…'

'Under the circumstances I think you'd better make it Gabe, don't you…?' A slow, intimate smile curved his beautifully cut lips. 'Or do you prefer Gabriel? I'm easy.'

So was I… The words sprang unbidden into Alice's mind.

The heat of humiliation surged once more in her cheeks. If he acted like this in front of other people he might just as well shout from the rooftops that they'd slept together. People weren't stupid. Someone, some time was bound to put two and two together and come up with Will! She struggled to keep the panic steadily building up inside under control.

'Just because your brother is happy—or maybe unhappy—to let you tell him what he thinks, don't think it works that way in other less dysfunctional families. Sophie has a mind of her own!' she choked.

'I'm glad to hear it,' Gabriel remarked drily. 'It's always useful if one person in a partnership has guts.'

'Do you always pull your brother to shreds like that?' Alice enquired critically.

'Only to his face, as a rule. Generally I lie through my teeth on his behalf, but as we're the next best thing to family I feel I can speak freely to you.'

Alice found herself wishing passionately he wouldn't.

'Family…? How do you make that out?' she asked, deeply alarmed at this theory.

'Greg is my half-brother; the mum-to-be is your sister. We're going to share a nephew-stroke-niece. In my book that makes us family.'

'They might not decide to marry.'

His impatient shrug suggested she was missing the obvious. 'There'll still be a baby. Being a father carries with it responsibilities. Greg will want to support them, both financially and practically. He's not the one carrying the baby but no man wants to be a stranger to his own child.'

Alice had heard of one or two who wouldn't have minded at all. She was surprised and disturbed by the vehemence in Gabriel's voice as he expressed these sentiments—ones *he* obviously meant. She found herself experiencing an inconvenient pang of guilt and ruthlessly suppressed it… The circumstances were not comparable.

'Does *Greg* know this? Or haven't you told him yet?'

'Listen, I know you don't like Greg—'

'Do *you*?' she interrupted sharply.

'Not always,' he admitted. His slow, reflective smile held a rueful affection that softened his features. 'But I do love the kid, and despite being spoilt from the day he drew breath he's basically a good guy. Sure, he panicked when he found out about the baby. But he wouldn't be the first. Personally, I think marriage with the right sort of girl is just what he needs…'

'You mean if he's got a wife she might keep him out of trouble and save you a lot of hassle?' she accused scornfully.

'That thought had occurred to me.'

'If you were trying to sell me Greg as a brother-in-law you haven't done much of a job so far!'

'Why would I want to sell you anything, Alice? I thought you were all for leaving the young people to sort it out for themselves.'

Alice gave an exasperated snort. 'I'd think I'd have preferred it if you'd thought Sophie was a gold-digger!' she exclaimed.

'That was always one possibility,' Gabriel admitted readily, 'but, having heard Greg's version of events, I think there's only one victim here, and it isn't my brother.' His voice carried a grimness that made Alice appreciate just why Greg might be afraid of his brother.

There had been nothing grudging in his candid admission, and she felt confused and simultaneously suspicious of his apparent forthrightness.

'In Greg's defence I have to say I've never seen him this smitten by a girl, and he doesn't usually go for teenagers.' His expression suggested that personally he found this attraction impossible to understand. 'If your sister loves him I think the responsibility might well be the making of him… Does she?'

One dark brow quirked at a quizzical angle, he gave her a direct look that Alice found impossible to wriggle away from. Actually, she felt as if his eyes were pinning her to the wall. He'd pinned her to the wall that night, only not with his eyes…

The sudden freeze-frame image in her head filled her with intense shame—the silhouette of two bodies as close to being one as it was possible to get… How did I behave like that? She pulled at the neckline of her tee-shirt fretfully.

'I don't know.' Her voice had a hoarse, strained quality as she struggled to put the past where it belonged. 'Sophie has gone away to think.'

'And what will she decide?' he persisted.

'You don't get it, do you?' She gave him an exasperated scowl. 'You might tell your brother what to think, but Sophie is no puppet. I'll just try and support her in her decision.'

'A commendable attitude.' He seemed noticeably unimpressed. 'What if that decision is to marry Greg? Will your non-interventionist policy hold true then?'

'Even then,' she confirmed reluctantly.

'Greg thinks you're trying to spike his guns. He finds you scary.'

'I think Greg finds anyone scary who doesn't respond to his charm, and I'm not the sort of person who is won over by a slick tongue and a pretty face.'

Gabriel's dark eyes narrowed as he digested her lofty claim.

'I'm left wondering just what it was about me that won you over that memorable night.' At his soft words all the colour leached from Alice's face.

Knowing that what was coming next was inevitable, she watched his brow furrow in mock confusion before his eyes abruptly widened with comic comprehension. Alice started as he vigorously slapped his thigh.

'Don't tell me…!' he instructed firmly. 'It was my inner goodness shining through again, wasn't it?'

'You think you're so clever, don't you?' she hissed. She'd known he'd be determined to mortify her. He didn't know that he couldn't think anything about her she hadn't already thought herself.

'Well, you'd know about stupid men, wouldn't you? As you're married to a prize idiot!'

'Leave Oliver out of this!' she yelled.

'Or do you have his tacit approval of your nocturnal activities? Perhaps you share the details with him later… Some men get off on that sort of thing, I understand.'

'You're *sick*!'

The soft noise Alice hadn't noticed emerging from the intercom became a sudden wail.

'My son needs me,' she said shakily. 'Why don't you let yourself out? Incidentally, if I have got any influence with Sophie I'll use it to stop her getting any more involved with someone who's even remotely connected with you!'

Gabriel appeared to take her open malice in his stride. 'At least you've dropped all that objectivity rubbish. We both know where we stand, I think.'

Pushing past him, Alice wished she could say the same. In the last half-hour her whole life had been turned upside-down!

CHAPTER TWO

'I WONDER what are they up to. Big brother must want to give me the once-over, probably, and warn me off. Perhaps,' she theorised a little wildly, 'he'll want to pay me off.'

Alice knew better than to interrupt Sophie in the midst of one of her wilder flights of fancy. She maintained a neutral silence; she didn't feel in the mood to get involved in convoluted conspiracy theories.

'If he's having his brother there, I want you. I'm not about to be browbeaten.'

Privately Alice didn't think she'd ever seen anyone *less* browbeaten. She was the one feeling helpless. She'd seen that stubborn set of her sister's chin before.

She *could* have said, I can't possibly come with you because Gabriel MacAllister is the father of my child and he doesn't know. That might prove distracting, she brooded darkly. And oh, incidentally, I don't want him to know! It brought a wry fleeting smile to her face when she imagined how her sister would respond to that dynamite confession! God, how did my life get this complicated?

Naturally she was glad that Sophie had returned from the long weekend break at their grandmother's house outside York in a positive frame of mind, but an energised Sophie was hard to resist once she set her mind on something!

And it was Alice who had convinced her she ought to speak to the wretched boy! She repressed a cowardly impulse to look for the nearest bucket of sand to bury her head in!

Drinks with the MacAllister brothers was not exactly her idea of a restful evening. It might have been a less daunting prospect on neutral ground, but it seemed Gabriel had leased Milborne Hall on the outskirts of town.

Alice had been forced to listen to local speculation about this surprising development for the past two days. She found herself praying that the more optimistic amongst the locals were wrong when they said rather smugly it was perfectly natural Gabriel MacAllister would want to live somewhere as perfect as their little rural backwater.

'Wouldn't it be better if Mum and Dad…?'

'*Are you kidding!* Mum starts crying every time I look at her, and I'm just glad Dad sold his shotgun last year,' Sophie reflected grimly. 'You can laugh…'

Not recently!

'But you're not living there. I wish I'd stayed at Gran's.'

'I'm working…' Alice made a feeble last-ditch attempt to wriggle out of it.

'You're not on duty until nine, are you…?' Sophie smiled when her sister glumly nodded. 'Fine, drop Will off a couple off hours early with Mum and we'll go straight there. We'll be finished in plenty of time for you to get to work. Anyone would think you were the one scared of meeting the man! It's not you he's gunning for.'

No, but he would be if he ever found out, Alice reflected grimly. But he never would. This line didn't contain the same comforting certainty it once had when she'd lain awake in the night wondering if she'd done the right thing letting everyone assume… They'd all been so pleased and supportive. It had been the idea of Oliver's baby—her great-grandson—that had kept Olivia, his grandmother, going after the devastating news of her grandson's death. Of course she'd done the right thing—the only thing, she reassured herself briskly.

'I'm sure Mr MacAllister is not *gunning* for you, Sophie.'

'He'll either think I'm just a feckless kid who got out of her depth, or I'm using the oldest trick in the book to get a rich meal ticket.' Her carefully nurtured hard-boiled expression was spoiled by the quiver of her soft lips.

'I'm sure he won't think anything of the sort, and even if he does, five seconds after he's seen you he'll know different,' Alice responded crisply. 'Besides, what does it matter what *he* thinks of you?'

'In a perfect world it wouldn't,' Sophie admitted, sounding very mature and even a little bit cynical to Alice's sensitive ears. 'Didn't you like him?' she added shrewdly, regarding her normally placid sister's belligerent expression curiously. 'You haven't told me much about what he said.'

'There isn't much to tell.' She was amazed and relieved that Sophie couldn't hear the guilt in her voice.

'And was he as good-looking as they say?'

'Better, probably,' Alice admitted after a reluctant pause during which an image of Gabriel's dark lean features rose up to mock her. 'And I'm sure he'd be the first to tell you so,' she reflected with sweet malice.

Sophie laughed. 'That's probably where Greg gets it from,' she concluded ruefully. 'He takes longer than me to get ready, and I've not known him to pass a mirror without checking himself out.'

Alice instinctively knew the comparison was unfair, and had to bite her tongue to prevent herself springing, quite inappropriately, to Gabriel's defence. You couldn't compare her sister's lover's narcissistic love affair with his own reflection with Gabriel's impregnable confidence. Gabriel's innate arrogance was such that he didn't need the designer accessories to bolster his self-worth.

* * *

Alice double-checked the pocket of her light jacket. Fortunately Sophie had been too preoccupied to notice that her big sister was as jumpy as a kitten.

'I've left my mobile in the car.' She clicked her tongue in exasperation and frowned as her sister rang the doorbell.

'Don't panic. I'll get it.' Sophie was halfway down the shallow steps that led to the entrance of the sprawling Victorian pile before Alice could respond.

She didn't like the necessity of leaving Will, not even with her mother. Even though it was only two nights a week, she made sure she could always be contacted. Considering her mother's age, she wasn't sure how fair it was to her, or how much longer the arrangement would work, but that was a problem for the future. She had plenty more immediate ones to occupy her mind at the moment!

Money wasn't a *major* problem yet, but since a couple of Oliver's more chancy investments had gone bad the hours she put in at the hospital were a big help, and when Will was eventually in school and the time came for her to resume her career full-time it would be an advantage that she wasn't totally out of touch.

It was a smartly dressed pleasant-looking woman who came to the door. Alice assumed she was the housekeeper; the MacAllisters were the sort of people who had housekeepers, chauffeurs and probably food-tasters too, she decided grimly. She couldn't be the only person who wished Gabriel was safely out of the picture—she instinctively knew he would make a formidable business adversary.

Before either she or the older woman had had a chance to speak, Gabriel was there.

'Thanks, Mrs Croft, I'll see to this. Come in, Alice…

Said the spider to the fly…she thought, obeying the command thinly disguised as an invitation. She'd only ever seen him in a formal suit—or nothing at all—before. It had been a bad idea to recall the 'nothing at all' part! Today he was wearing pale-coloured jeans, that emphasised his ultra-slim hips and endless legs, teamed with an open-necked black polo shirt.

Even when she stepped up from the lower step he still towered over her. Despite the fact she'd stepped out of the sun her body was abruptly bathed in an uncomfortable heat.

Gabriel had to be used to the stock female reaction of open-mouthed appreciation. He probably accepted such admiration as nothing more than his due, she thought sourly. Perhaps it was far too late not to be obvious, but Alice didn't want to be classed with the adoring masses. She kept her own mouth firmly shut, even when her squirming insides were swallowed up by a deep dark hole.

His features were not nearly as classically perfect as his half brother's, his nose might even be classed beaky by the envious, but he had a raw sex appeal that went clear off the scale. Alice's eyes touched his wide sensual mouth and she gave a little shudder that had nothing whatever to do with disgust!

Alice was angered by her obvious display of weakness, but decided the best way to deal with it was to pretend it hadn't happened. He probably hadn't noticed; he wasn't even looking at her.

'Where is your sister?'

Horror swept over Alice. Reprehensibly, she'd forgotten about Sophie, who arrived at that moment dead on cue. She looked sweet, sexy and wholesome. Alice avoided looking at Gabriel's face; she didn't particularly want to see the boringly predictable male response this dynamite combination inevitably inspired in men. It was then that she noticed for the first time Sophie was looking from her to Gabriel and back again with a stunned expression.

'Are you unwell?' Gabriel had obviously noticed too.

Sophie tipped her head back to look up at the tall dark man. 'I'm fine,' she said hoarsely, licking her dry lips. 'It's crazy, but seeing you standing there with Alice, I thought...from a distance you looked so like Oliver.'

Just shut up...*please*... I should have foreseen this possibility, Alice thought, feeling the panic that had been her constant companion since her dark anonymous lover had acquired a name rise dangerously close to the surface.

'Oliver?' He looked distressingly alert.

'Alice's husband.' Sophie stepped into the hallway, her soft hair a bright focus against sombre panelling and attractive dark William Morris wallpaper. 'It felt like someone just walked over my grave,' she confessed with a theatrical shudder.

'And does seeing...Oliver always make you look so distressed?'

'He's dead,' Sophie said, glancing apologetically towards Alice.

Gabriel's dark eyes moved automatically to Alice. The light dusting of blusher along her high cheekbones stood out starkly against the pallor of her pale, blemishless skin.

'It was only from a distance, when I was over by the car. Up close you're nothing alike.'

'I'm very sorry.'

If Sophie hadn't been there she'd have told him where he could shove his insincerity. Alice inclined her head coldly in acknowledgement.

'Is this bereavement recent?'

'Nearly three years ago,' Sophie said, when her sister continued to stare at Greg's brother with a peculiarly intense animosity. She'd never seen Alice behave like this towards anyone before. Perhaps it hadn't been such a good idea to bring her after all.

The housekeeper appeared and their host turned aside to

speak to her. Sophie took the opportunity to hiss warningly at her sister.

'There's no point antagonising him. I'm not asking you to sleep with the man... Joke, Ally, don't be such a prude,' she said in an impatient undertone when her sister went bright scarlet. 'But he is pretty delicious,' she mused in an admiring undertone. Don't you think? I hope you don't mind I brought my sister. You've met, I believe,' she added as the housekeeper moved away oozing quiet efficiency.

Gabriel MacAllister briefly took the hand she held out but seemed to lose interest almost immediately.

Considering she'd been expecting to be the subject of a microscopic examination herself, it struck Sophie as ironic that she was being virtually ignored. Perhaps he was lulling her into a false sense of security? A frown pleated her smooth young brow as she looked questioningly towards her sister.

Alice didn't notice the look. Sophie thought it was entirely possible her sister had forgotten she was there at all. Then it came to her. *Of course*—she wasn't the only one to see the similarity. Poor Alice, she thought compassionately, no wonder she can't take her eyes off him. It didn't explain why he couldn't take his eyes off her, of course... *Unless...?*

A speculative light entered her blue eyes to be closely followed by a worried gleam. Alice needed a man, but not one like this! He was just too...just too much *everything* she decided, examining this spectacular specimen of manhood with a worried expression. According to Greg he didn't lack female companionship. She'd have to think of a way to casually drop details of his ladykilling reputation into the conversation with Alice.

'Greg's waiting in the drawing room.' Gabriel nodded his dark head towards a half-open door.

Sophie moved forward before turning back uncertainly when Gabriel made no attempt to follow her.

'Aren't you coming? I thought it was to be…' she began betrayingly.

'Thumbscrews…?' Gabriel suggested with an expressive quirk of one dark brow. His wry grin broadened as the young girl blushed. 'I see my reputation precedes me,' he murmured drily. 'We'll join you later.'

Heart thudding sickeningly, Alice listened to the awful inevitability of that *we*. Gabriel MacAlllister was the last person in the world she wanted to be classed as *we* with. She tried hard to respond to Sophie's nervous grin as she vanished.

'Would you like to see the garden?'

Impersonal, polite… No need to panic; polite conversation she could deal with. Sophie hadn't given away any vital information. He'd have been bound to learn she was a widow eventually if he stayed around the area.

'I believe you have a fine collection of old English roses here,' she responded stiltedly.

'Have we?' The offhand shrug of his broad shoulders displayed not a scrap of interest in horticultural heritage as he placed a light but insistent hand against her shoulder-blade. 'I wouldn't know. We do have very old English plumbing, though,' he supplied helpfully. 'It precedes the building by several centuries. I suspect it came over with William the Conqueror. Charming, if you like cold showers.'

It wasn't a question of like, more *need* she concluded, tearing her eyes from his hawkishly perfect profile. The sweat not absorbed by her light cotton bra had pooled uncomfortably in the rounded hollow between her breasts. The tingling in her nipples made her acutely conscious of the area.

Alice gave a condescending sniff. When the going got tough, some people headed straight back to their air-conditioning and indoor pools—well, she could hope, couldn't she?

'Why did you lease the place, then, if it's s...sub-standard?'

'I didn't...well, only on Greg's behalf. There's a dearth of rentable property around here, and I persuaded him purchasing might be a bit premature. He thinks becoming a householder will give him gravitas and convince your sister of his good intentions.'

'She probably won't be so impressed if she knows you're paying the bill.' Alice was gently panting as she reached a near trot. His long legs were making very few concessions to her less impressive limbs.

'Oh, I don't know. She struck me as a very sensible sort of girl.' He came to such an abrupt stop she almost bumped into him.

Hands outstretched, anticipating a collision, Alice found her palms slapping up against his chest.

'S...sorry,' she stammered, after a telltale gap of total immobility.

A gap during which panic and something far more sinister had uncoiled hotly in the pit of her belly. His short-sleeved polo shirt was fine knitted cotton and she could almost feel the texture of the dark curling hair that lightly covered his broad chest.

Her tingling fingertips felt remarkably reluctant to relinquish the contact as she drew jerkily back.

'Here'll do, I think.'

'Do for what?'

He got straight to the point. 'Why didn't you tell me on Friday that you were a widow?'

'Why…?' It wasn't hard under the circumstances to assume a dumb expression. She felt slow and stupid.

'Like it didn't come up in the conversation.' He drawled. His languid tone was not reflected in his face; he looked remarkably angry in a dark, dangerous broody had sort of way. 'I was slagging the guy off, if you recall.'

She did. 'I don't go around explaining details of my personal life to perfect strangers,' she replied with studied defiance.

This angry statement struck Gabriel as being bizarre—under the circumstances. His eyes darkened as some of the personal details he did know about her came to mind—like the tiny oval mole on her left shoulder and the silver appendix scar just below the shapely crest of her right hip.

'Even when you've shared your body with that perfect stranger?' His mobile lips formed a cruel parody of a smile.

There were perfect strangers and *perfect*, as in flawless strangers, Alice thought, her eyes reluctantly studying the angular perfection of his lean face. Did he think she was likely to forget?

'That was a long time ago,' she said in a hushed voice.

'About as long as your husband's death?' And was the tragic expression in her wide eyes reserved for that event or sleeping with him?

Alice's shoulders hunched forward defensively, but she just shook her head mutely.

'Do I look like him?' Glancing quickly up, she saw his expression suggested he didn't much care for this idea. His sharp cheekbones jutted through the tightly stretched smooth olive skin of his face. He had the sort of bone structure that would make a sculptor automatically reach for his chisel.

'Not really.'

'Your sister seemed to think…'

'Superficially, perhaps!' she snapped. 'You're the same height, build, and similar colouring.'

'Is that why you were looking at me that night? Because you thought I was him?' He took hold of her shoulders and Alice looked helplessly up at him.

'For a second,' she admitted, hoping he'd let the damned subject drop, but not getting her hopes up. He was the sort of person who could extract the last drop of blood from the most uncooperative stone. 'I suppose I *wanted* you to be him,' she reflected, with a frown.

Didn't everyone want to go back and say the things they wanted to say—unsay the things they wished they hadn't? Would she ever forget or forgive herself for those savage sentiments? The last things she'd ever said to Oliver.

Gabriel's chest lifted as he inhaled deeply. His expression had grown curiously still.

'How long had you been widowed?' His eyes were now focused on a point over her head.

'It was the day of the funeral.'

Gabriel gave a harsh, incredulous gasp before he let go of her shoulders. Alice watched him walk up to a large yew tree. He rubbed one finger slowly down the coarse-textured bark before turning abruptly back to face her.

'You used me.' It was an incredulous statement, not a question.

She gave a low, disbelieving grunt. 'You can dish it up, but you can't take it. Is that the problem here?' She found this classic display of male double standards staggering. He glared at her in brooding irritation. 'What were you doing to me if it wasn't using?'

'Don't you remember?' Wouldn't that be the final irony, he reflected grimly, when he could recall every touch, every erotic little catch of breath.

Gabriel wasn't entirely sure why he felt this angry—this

betrayed. It had only been a one-night stand, but then that was only half the truth too. One night it might have been, but it was *the* one night by which his every potential sexual encounter would be measured in the future, and found wanting. He knew this for a fact.

No woman had ever responded to him as she had, with such uninhibited pleasure. Every man probably had a fantasy lover, but few ever met them in the flesh—perhaps, he reflected grimly, they were the lucky ones!

After three years he could still hear her husky sobs of pleasure as he'd touched her and she'd touched him. He could recall the precise erotic journey her skilful fingers and lips had made over his skin. She'd displayed an insatiable curiosity for his body and what pleased him…what made him wild. His eyes darkened and his body responded helplessly to the memory. Gabriel didn't like being a helpless victim of his own lusts.

Now he didn't even have the illusion that it had been him she'd been moaning or begging for. She'd been closing her eyes and thinking of another man. Only her eyes hadn't been closed; they'd been wide open and deep drowning cornflower-blue.

The glazed, almost other-worldly quality in her expression seemed suddenly all too explicable. He'd been a macabre substitute! She'd been laying a ghost—quite literally!

The next time she'd know *exactly* who it was she was making love to, he vowed grimly. She'd been his totally that night and she would be again. The next time he was going to make her admit it.

'I do have a hazy recall.'

Gabriel's sharp inhalation made Alice regret her aggressively flippant response.

'I was hurting. I wanted someone to hold me.' That was only half the story, but she wasn't about to go into any of the painful details. As for her motivation—even after three years she hadn't quite fathomed that one out herself. There were some things that were better left well alone.

'We did a lot more than hold.'

A sudden light gust of wind blew her fine hair around her face and made the fine georgette blouse she wore billow softly. The material lifted it exposed the gentle indentation just above her navel. Her skin was smooth as silk and creamy pale.

'One thing led to another...' she reflected miserably. Glancing up, she saw his dark eyes were fixed on the small exposed area of skin around her midriff, and the restless, hungry expression she glimpsed made her swallow nervously. 'I'm not proud...' She pulled her jacket tight at the waist and told herself only a fool would find such dangerous scrutiny stimulating.

Gabriel's jaw tightened. Now that made him feel one hell of a lot better!

'We didn't work up to anything. The way I recall it we started at the top,' he growled bluntly, 'and stayed there.'

Alice's fractured sigh was audible.

Good! She remembered all right, he thought, savagely pleased to see confirmation in the faint distressed quivering movements of her long sensitive fingers.

The door had closed and she had pressed her fingers to his lips. 'Don't talk,' she'd pleaded.

She hadn't wanted to think; she had just wanted to feel—feel something that she'd instinctively known would blank out the pain and fill the emptiness within her. She had boldly delivered herself up into the hands of a total stranger, but oddly that hadn't frightened her.

He hadn't spoken—not then. They'd both been too impatient to even undress the first time. She'd ripped ineffectually at his clothes in the grip of a lustful frenzy like nothing she'd ever experienced before.

The piercing pleasure of that first kiss, the extraordinary, indescribable mixture of lust and tenderness, had made her go as limp as a rag doll. Gabriel had supported her then, displaying a virile strength that had excited her deeply. The need within her as he'd pressed his hard, aroused body up against hers had been immediate and total.

In total contrast to that swift, urgent coupling Gabriel had undressed her later with agonising slowness. He'd made up for his previous silence too, telling her as he peeled off each garment exactly what he was going to do to her and what she was going to do in return. Even as his insidiously sexy voice had dripped like honey all over her Alice hadn't quite been able to believe that people said such things! By the time she'd been naked Alice had been in a state of agonised arousal, almost begging him— Who was she kidding? She *had* begged him!

'That wasn't me…' she protested weakly. Am I trying to convince him or myself? she wondered.

'No?' He reached out and ran a finger down the length of her neatly trimmed hair. The pad of his fingertip rested briefly on the curve of her jaw before falling away. 'Despite the puritanical haircut, you look remarkably similar.'

'You know what I mean.' The casual contact had butterflies running riot in her belly. This is sexual deprivation talking, Alice Lynn, she told herself severely. Pull yourself together!

She'd been too involved with Will, and a lot of the time simply too tired from the demands of this solo job to admit she had any needs that weren't being met. Her body was letting her know just how wrong she'd been with a vengeance right now. It had been bound to happen some time—only not now, *please*, not with him!

'You were there in body but not in spirit,' Gabriel suggested with a sneer. 'Actually,' he leered, 'it's the body I'm interested in.'

'Tell me something I don't know.' She was obviously certifiable to find such a crudely phrased intent a turn-on.

Alice gasped when without warning his fingers curled in the shiny bangs of hair either side of the perfect oval of her face. He lowered his face down to her level, angling her face upwards and bringing his nose within an inch of her own.

'You were mine body and soul that night. Deny it if you can!'

'I'm warning you, I had garlic for lunch—lashings of it.' Eyes screwed up tight, she issued this dire warning from between clenched teeth. It was the best form of defence she could come up with at short notice, and she wasn't surprised to feel the sudden vibration of silent laughter in his chest.

If he kissed her she didn't know what she'd do, but she could hazard a fairly accurate guess. It was the guesswork, that and the fragrant warmth of his breath, that was in danger of turning her into a gibbering wreck.

For Will's sake she had to keep him at arm's length, no matter how attractive she found him. Or is it for *my* sake? a cynical voice in the back of her mind inconveniently asked. Didn't her son have the right to know who his real father was? Didn't a man have the right to know he had a son? No! He hadn't had procreation on his mind when he'd invited a total stranger to share his bed.

'You say the most seductive things, angel.'

'I'm not an angel.'

'That's a weight off my mind.'

'Why are you doing this?' He must have plenty of women, why the hell did he want her?

'Because you were the best sex I've ever had,' he told her frankly.

When her shocked eyes flickered open she found Gabriel looked inexplicably angry, as though he resented the admission he'd just made.

Alice was finding it hard to breathe properly. Had she really been that hot?

'Do you always say exactly what you're thinking?' There was no sign of tenderness in his austerely beautiful face to soften the stark honesty of his comment. Irrelevantly she noted that his lashes were the thickest and lushest she'd ever seen on a man. Her son would have those lashes when he was older, and the eyes too.

He laughed then, and it was a dangerously attractive sound—almost as attractive as the flash of very white even teeth in his dark face.

'If I did that I might get arrested, or maybe my face slapped. Or maybe not…?' He speculated. 'The fact is,' he said, allowing his thumbs to move in a soft, exploratory fashion over the angle of her firm jawline, 'everything since that night has been a bit of an anticlimax—in the bedroom department. I told myself if I ever met you again I'd take you to bed for a week—a month—however long it took to get you out of my system. Until today I thought you were married…'

'And that made a difference,' she grated hoarsely.

He really was absolutely *incredible*! Gabriel came right out and said things other people would blush to even think! *A week!* Her ribs felt in imminent danger of disintegration as her heart pounded thunderously within her tight chest. *A month!* The very idea! She felt sick—she felt *something!*

'We've all got our little moral hang-ups,' he murmured regretfully.

'Some of us less than others,' she responded faintly.

She couldn't believe he had the gall to talk about morals! But then her membership of the moral high ground was distinctly shaky under the circumstances, she recalled reluctantly.

'You shouldn't beat yourself up about our one-night stand,' he soothed, ladling on the sardonic understanding with a heavy hand.

'I wasn't talking about me!' she hissed.

'You're not as tall as I remembered.'

'Sorry,' she responded ironically. She'd probably disappoint him in a lot of other ways too. Not that she was going to put herself in a position where he could match his memories to reality.

'No criticism implied. Only when we made love the first time—'

'Had sex,' she snapped. There had been no mention of love when he'd said she was the best sex he'd ever had! She listened with dismay to the unmistakable sound of bitterness in her own voice.

'You were wearing those high heels. Now you're not wearing anything nearly as sexy—in the shoe department, that is.'

She would have glanced automatically towards her sensibly shod feet if he hadn't had other ideas. As far as Gabriel was concerned she was looking at him until he decided otherwise.

She flushed angrily at her own passive acceptance of this restraint. Anyone would think she was enjoying it. It was about time she made it quite clear this was definitely not the case!

'Let me go!'

'Kiss me, and I'll think about it. I'm willing to risk the garlic…'

It terrified her to realise how attractive she might have

found this offer had the circumstances been entirely different.

'You know you want to,' he taunted softly. His eyes rested pointedly on the prominent outline of her nipples as they chafed against the thin layers of her clothes.

It was then Alice kicked him hard on the shins. He was crude, vile and unforgivably correct about her feelings. She heard him grunt in pain as she turned and began to run. She'd only taken a couple of strides before a hand on her shoulder swung her around.

'The offer still stands,' he said, wrapping one arm firmly around her ribcage.

His chest was rising, though not as rapidly as her own, which gave the impression she'd just done five thousand metres not five.

It would be undignified to struggle, not to mention pointless. There was only one way to prove to him that she wasn't the person he remembered—not really. That night had been the result of a set of freak circumstances; it couldn't be repeated.

Oliver had been her only lover until his death. They'd had an enjoyable sex life, familiar, pleasant and comfortingly predictable, at least until that dreadful last year, but it had never been going to set the world alight. She wasn't that sort of person.

She grabbed a handful of his shirt to steady herself, hooked one hand behind his neck and tugged his head down. She placed her lips firmly against his mouth with every intention until the final moment of contact to withdraw almost immediately.

That was before a depth charge went off in her nervous system. The electrical flash extended all the way down to her curling toes. With a humiliating lack of hesitation, which she would later reflect upon bitterly, she accepted—

even *welcomed*—the lustful lunge of his tongue into the moist recesses of her mouth.

The texture of his lips, the taste of him, the marvellous proximity of his hard, lean, *aroused* body was a heady cocktail of sheer undiluted erotic bliss.

'This is terrible!' she gasped when, true to his word, Gabriel released her. Alice hugged her arms around herself protectively.

Gabriel raked a hand through his thick sleek dark hair. For once he didn't appear to have a slick retort to hand.

'Why terrible?' Alice didn't notice that he sounded distracted.

'Because I liked it.'

Gabriel smiled and let the tepid *like* pass. 'So did I.'

She'd noticed, but she tried not to do so too obviously now, as she struggled to keep her fraught gaze on his face. The hot melting sensation between her thighs didn't dissipate even when good taste won out over crude desire.

'Is that a bad thing?'

'I don't do casual sex.' The sardonic quirk of one eyebrow made her flush. 'Normally.'

'Neither do I…normally.' Gabriel had never felt less casual in his life.

'I have a son.'

'Keep this quiet, only mothers *have* been known to have sex,' he told her in sarcastic hushed undertones.

'Not this one,' she responded unthinkingly, with such feeling that he gave a deep growl of laughter. 'I didn't mean it like…' she faltered, biting her lips in vexation. What a time to be spontaneous!

'Then how did you mean it?'

Gabriel watched as she opened her mouth several times—he could think of worse things to look at than the full soft outline—in an attempt to place a less controversial interpretation on her words before eventually lapsing into a pink-cheeked resentful silence.

'Your last time was with me, wasn't it?' He wasn't a vain man, but he couldn't repress a strong surge of complacency.

'I'm not in the market for an affair.'

'After three years?'

He made it sound extraordinary that she'd lasted three minutes. What did he think she was—a sex junkie? Taking into account how she'd behaved that night, Alice realised as a fresh wave of horror submerged her that that was *exactly* what he was likely to think.

'Celibacy seems remarkably attractive when the alternative is sex with you!'

'A challenge?' he enquired silkily, looking in no way disturbed by her rash declaration.

He sounded as though he'd enjoy making her retract her claim. The bad part was she knew that he could.

'No, it wasn't,' she admitted stiltedly, already regretting her reckless response.

'You lashed out—I make you panic.' The air of benevolent understanding didn't sit easily with the prowling hunger in his eyes. 'I wonder why?'

Alice exhaled noisily. 'You can ask that? You calmly say you're going to take me to bed for a week and I'm supposed to be calm. *Panic!*' she squeaked indignantly. 'Anyone would panic.' She paused and drew breath into her hungry lungs.

'I can think of several people of the female variety who would be flattered, at the very least.'

'You're so full of yourself,' she jeered, examining the complacency of his thin-lipped smile with growing dislike. He was the sort of man to whom things—including women—*especially* women—had always come far too easily.

And I didn't exactly break the trend, did I?

The slow smile that that spread across his face was devilish. She couldn't understand why she hadn't noticed his similarity to the guy with the pointy tail before.

'I think I'd prefer it if you were full of me. I think you would too.'

It was a full twenty seconds before the scandalous imagery of this crude, shocking statement hit her. 'I...you...' she choked.

The desire that ran through her veins was hot and thick. She had obviously lost all sense of decency, she concluded, horrified by the tingling currents of excitement created by the abrupt hormonal overload. Her breasts were straining against her thin bra; her body was almost audibly humming with mindless desire.

The thick veils of dark lashes brushed against the high crest of his cheekbones and Gabriel's nostrils flared.

'As one,' he agreed throatily, looking directly at her.

She cleared her throat noisily. If she fell in heap now he'd think she made a habit of it. It wasn't easy to remain upright.

'I suppose you think talking like that is a turn-on!' she sneered.

'I can only speak for myself. And you can probably see for yourself how turned on I am.'

Alice gave a mortified little moan. 'You're the most vulgar man I've ever met!' It was a struggle after what he'd said to keep her eyes on his face.

She brought her teeth together with a jarring suddenness when he inclined his dark head slowly, as if acknowledging a compliment.

'We should be talking about Sophie and Greg.'

Gabriel recognised full retreat when he saw it, but he wasn't about to press his advantage. He'd waited three years and he was satisfied with the progress he'd made today.

Some sort of sister I am, Alice reflected. I should be thinking about Sophie, not lusting after this appalling man.

'Personally I'm in need of a break from Sophie—and especially Greg,' he announced heartlessly. 'But if you really want to we can join them for coffee…'

'I can't.' She glanced at the slim metallic watch on her wrist. 'I'll be late if I don't leave.'

'Late for what?' He looked disgruntled by this announcement.

'Work.' Alice felt childishly pleased she'd spoiled his plans.

'At this hour! What about your son?'

She thought she could hear a critical edge in his tone and her chin went up.

'I don't actually think my childcare arrangements are any of your business.'

'What do you do?'

'I'm a nurse at the local community hospital.'

There were no resident medical staff in the small casualty department, just an on-call GP. They only dealt with the simplest of emergencies and referred the rest to the bigger hospitals in the city.

'Nurse.' His brows lifted in surprise. 'Yes,' he mused thoughtfully. 'I can see you as a nurse.'

'Well, I hope you don't—not professionally speaking, that is.'

'I'm touched by your concern for my health and well-being.'

'I was just thinking you'd make an awful patient. The

sort that makes sleazy comments about sexy uniforms and shoves his hand up your skirt,' she told him venomously.

Actually, if Gabriel appeared as a patient he'd probably be the one on the receiving end of flirtatious advances, she thought, dismissing the professional detachment of her colleagues with an angry frown. She felt a sharp stab of jealousy as she mentally surveyed this imaginary scene.

His smile faded abruptly. 'Good God! You don't have to put up with things like that, do you?' he demanded austerely.

Whilst Gabriel certainly would have liked to slide his hands over the smooth curve of her thigh, the thought of other men—men who in his imagination had crude lascivious leers on their faces—wanting to do the same made his chest swell with deep affront. He saw no inconsistency in his attitude.

His unexpected reaction struck Alice as being curious. 'What things…?' It took her a second to refocus her wandering thoughts. 'Oh, no, not very often. And actually some of us wear trousers these days.'

She fished her phone from her pocket.

'What are you doing?'

'I came in Sophie's car; mine is off the road.' A frown furrowed her brow as she thought of this major inconvenience. 'I said I'd get a taxi into work.' She gave a frustrated grimace when she heard the engaged tone.

'I'll take you.'

CHAPTER THREE

'THAT'S very kind of you…' Alice began after a few seconds of horrified silence. She stopped, aware of how stupid she sounded. 'No, no, you're not kind.'

Looking into his liquid dark eyes and watching the intriguing amber lights in the velvet depths made her stomach muscles twist hard enough to make her bite back the small tell-tale gasp. Her self-respect winced at this further reminder of how stupidly susceptible she was to Gabriel's unique brand of bold sensuality.

'You're not the first person to make that observation,' he admitted frankly.

'Well, that's nothing to boast about,' she told him severely. 'And I'd prefer to walk.' She couldn't afford to breathe the same air as him, let alone enclose herself in something as confined as a car.

'I'm not too hot on local geography yet, but I'd say that's a good three miles?'

'I didn't say I'm *going* to walk. I said I'd *prefer* to walk.'

'You were making a point. The point being you'd prefer blisters to my company. I'm hurt.'

'If only that were true.' This was beginning to get childish, she decided, responding to his mocking smile with a sniff. She shook the phone impatiently after she'd unsuccessfully redialled.

'Here come the young lovers,' he remarked, looking up the sweeping curve of the lawn beyond her. 'If not exactly hand in hand, they are together. What do you suppose that might mean?'

'I don't know or care!' she flashed, thoroughly harassed by this point. She wasn't acting like a responsible mother who put the welfare of her son above all else. She was acting like some sex-starved little tart!

'That sounded like an authentic let-them-get-on-with-it sentiment to me. It's good to see you're coming around to my way of thinking.'

'Hell would freeze over before I'd agree with you about anything!' she snapped.

'It's a pleasure to see objectivity at work.'

Suddenly she could see the appeal of her son's colourful tantrums—a recent trying stage in his development. Lying on the ground and kicking her heels might give some sort of relief from this awful situation.

'Sophie and I thought we might go out for a bite to eat,' Greg remarked warily when they were within hailing distance.

Alice arranged her face into a mask of strained composure before turning around. 'That's nice.'

Greg didn't see beyond the brilliance of her smile. He looked so surprised and gratified by her response that she wondered guiltily if she might not have been a little hard on him in the past.

'Sophie says you might need a lift to the hospital. We could…' he began eagerly.

It was such an obvious attempt to butter her up that Alice's smile wilted. At least Gabriel didn't try and sweet-talk her. She definitely preferred a more straightforward approach. Dear God, she thought, listening to her own thought processes with amazement, next I'll be saying Gabriel is a really *nice* guy! Pay attention, Alice! 'Nice' was a completely inappropriate adjective where he was concerned, and as for 'straightforward'—he was totally twisted and devious.

'No, that's fine, kids, off you go,' Gabriel put in swiftly, with an avuncular benevolence that made Alice want to scream. 'I've already offered to give Alice a lift.'

His benign smile taunted her to deny it as he waved his *fait accompli* under her angrily twitching nose.

'You're a sly, manipulative snake,' Alice observed through her fixed grin as she waved goodbye to her sister.

'I don't know why you're concerned. If it's any comfort to you I haven't made out in car for…oh, years,' he concluded, with a heavy nostalgic sigh for his dissipated youth.

She wasn't about to admit it wasn't *him* she didn't trust. But she was not going to do anything crazy or degrading. Restraint was all she needed.

'I think you're right to restrain yourself,' she sniffed. 'A man of a certain age can look a little foolish trying to ape a teenager.'

A grin sliced through the solemnity of his expression. 'Bitch,' he observed, almost affectionately.

'I take it I can rely upon your continued restraint,' she announced with cold formality.

How, she wondered, was she going to feel if he gave a negative response? Flinging herself from the moving car might be a bit on the dramatic side, so tensely she sank back into the luxurious pale leather upholstery and awaited his reply.

'I wouldn't like to commit myself on that one,' he confessed. 'I like to keep my options open.' The smile that tugged his lips into an attractive lopsided grin made it appear he quite enjoyed contemplating these options.

'Well, I'm one option that is firmly closed.' Don't even *think* about what it would be like, Alice.

'Admit it, you'd have been piqued if I'd categorically

said I wasn't going to make a pass,' he challenged her. 'All women like to think they're irresistible.'

Alice, who'd been going to maintain an icy silence, hooted in derision.

'You don't agree?' he enquired. 'Is it a left turn here?' he added, as they came to a fork in the narrow country lane.

'Left, and then left again at the telephone kiosk. When you say "like to think" that kind of implies they're not, but you're willing to humour them.'

'If you knew me better, Alice…'

'What a horrid prospect…' she muttered crossly.

'You'd know I never humour anyone,' he drawled, looking amused by her bad-tempered interruption.

One day with Will and he'd be eating his imperious words, she thought, deriving some pleasure from the idea of Will running rings around this arrogant word merchant.

'It's obvious you've never had a toddler,' she responded, without thinking.

'I hope not.' He flicked her a quick grin but was only rewarded with a side view of her chin. It was bright red as was her neck. What, he puzzled, had he done to spook her now?

What kind of idiot, she wondered, threw out a taunt like that to the father of her own son? It wasn't as if she'd forgotten, was it? It was almost inviting the sort of speculation she wanted to avoid at all costs.

'You and Greg don't look alike.' The desperation she felt to change the subject was clear in her overly bright tone.

Gabriel flicked her another thoughtful look. 'Even in my youth I was never boy band material,' he agreed sadly.

True. Pretty he was not; what he had was a raw sex

appeal that would survive the years a lot better than a pretty face.

She grunted scornfully. 'Speaking as one well past his sell-by date, I suppose.' Who was he kidding? He'd spent the last thirty-something years basking in female adulation and enjoying every minute!

'I'm sure your sister would agree with you.'

'Why, were you thinking of seducing her too?' she responded snappily, uneasily aware that Sophie would think no such thing. I am not jealous, she told herself. Such an idea was not conceivable.

'I didn't seduce you, Alice.' His deep voice held a silky sexy intonation that sent a shiver down between her clammy shoulderblades. 'In fact if anyone was a bit pushy it was you.'

Like I needed reminding of that! She pressed the button to release the window and turned her hot face to the rush of air. If he'd been any sort of gentleman he'd let it alone.

'I can adjust the air-conditioning if you're too hot.'

'I'm not hot. I just like fresh air.' Irritation had been interlaced with the teasing note in his voice. She had a fleeting impression he was impatient with the word-games. Did the truth start where word-games ended...? She wasn't ready for that yet...*never*! 'What half do you and Greg share, then? Mother or father?'

'You're very inquisitive.'

'What can I say?' She threw up her hands in exaggerated culpability. 'You're such a fascinating subject,' she told him waspishly.

'And when we're talking about me we can't be talking about you,' he mused intuitively. Alice turned wide, startled eyes on him and he granted her a glimpse of his wolfish smile before transferring his attention back to the road. 'Mother.'

'Pardon?'

'My mum married Greg's dad,' he explained patiently.

'Then how come,' she puzzled, 'you share a surname?'

'Robert MacAllister adopted me.'

'Did you mind about that...losing your father's name?'

'I didn't have a father until Mum married Robert. That isn't to say I was the product of an immaculate conception. My father just didn't stick around when he knew I was on the way.' His harsh voice was laden with scorn.

'Is that why...?' She stopped awkwardly.

'Why I want Greg to take an active part in fatherhood? You really don't give the guy much credit, do you, Alice? He's not at his best with you; you make him nervous.' Her eyes widened with shock as, startled, she spun around in her seat to look at him incredulously. Satisfied he'd made his point, Gabriel continued. 'True, *I* don't have much time for men who don't accept their responsibilities, but I didn't need to apply any pressure to Greg.'

His dry tone made her shift uneasily once more in her seat. It surprised her that Gabriel seemed genuinely unaware that he was the sort of person whom most people would think twice about disagreeing with. His leadership qualities were a little overdeveloped for her taste—unlike his body, which was just about perfect in the development department.

She gave a startled gasp. That wayward thought had sneakily crept up behind her defences.

'Maybe I was born with this strong sense of family... Who actually knows in retrospect how much impact our formative experiences have on our adult beliefs?'

Alice's jaw tightened defensively. 'But you do think a child without a father is missing out?' It was a subject that kept her awake at nights.

'It rather depends on the father. Would Oliver have made a good father?'

Alice stifled the sudden flurry of uncertainty this abrupt question created. 'Yes,' she replied firmly.

With a nod Gabriel accepted her reply, ironically more readily than she did herself. Oliver had desperately wanted a child, but he'd had a very idealised view of parenthood, and on the occasions when friends had visited with their youngsters he had never been able to wait for them to leave.

It would probably have been different with their own children, but she did occasionally wonder how he would have coped with the inevitable changes a child would have brought to their lifestyle. She'd always been the one to compromise in their relationship—a fact she had only recognised in hindsight. Parenthood, as she knew, was all about compromise and adaptability.

'Like my mum, you didn't have any choice in the matter.'

Well, that was true. At least in so far as you couldn't contact a father when you didn't even know his name! She'd never felt so guilty in her life!

'It's the ones who didn't have the situation thrust upon them I don't understand. The women who deliberately set out to bring up a child as single parent. I'm not saying your son isn't perfectly well balanced and I didn't consider myself disadvantaged as a child. My mother was so supremely self-sufficient and capable that I couldn't figure out why anyone needed the traditional family format.

'I didn't think what we had could be improved upon, and it took me quite a while to accept Robert, but he made an incredible difference to my life. After the initial resentment, not being the man of the house was quite a release. I could be a kid again. A child from a single parent background often grows up too fast...'

'This is it. We're here!' Her shoulders slumped in relief.

'Do you always sound so jubilant when you arrive at work?' he enquired drily as he pulled up in front of the red-brick building.

'I don't like to be late; it's unprofessional,' she told him coldly as she continued to wrestle with the door lever.

'I'll handle it,' he said, leaping agilely out of the car. With a courtly flourish he flung open the door. Alice greeted his gesture with deep suspicion. 'I really enjoyed our little chat,' he added as she emerged trying not to show how flustered she felt.

'From my point of view it's been a total waste of time.' Not to mention a nightmare.

'Perhaps I can do something about that?' The shivery sensation in her stomach seemed to anticipate his intentions before her brain had collated all the relevant details.

The second kiss proved what a very bad job she'd made of *not* remembering the first. His cool lips were every bit as skilful as she recalled and his tongue just as audacious. He tasted incredibly good. She could now recall the time his lips had tasted of *her*, and her groan was lost in his throat.

When his grip of the hair at the nape of her neck loosened and he drew back she gave a deep, dreamy sigh. Where was spitting outrage when a girl needed it? No wonder he looked so pleased with himself, the smug, complacent snake!

He rubbed the tip of her chin with his thumb. 'No, don't say a thing; it might spoil the moment, darling,' he told her with throaty mockery.

Alice snapped her head back and took the hand he'd clasped dramatically on his chest and shifted it. 'Your heart—and I'm giving the benefit of the doubt, here—is on the left side.'

'It's really encouraging to see how hot you are on anatomy…' His exaggerated leer just stopped short of salivating. 'Speaking as a potential patient, of course.'

'As for spoiling the moment!' she spluttered. 'I'd prefer to spoil your face!'

She stalked, head held high, into the building, the sound of his laughter ringing in her ears.

Unfortunately her arrival and the kiss had been witnessed by several curious colleagues, who were used to see her arrive in her old estate, not a large luxurious Merc.

It had given everyone—and you'd think people would have something better to do—the opportunity to assimilate Gabriel's stunning physical attributes. They wanted all the gruesome details, and when she assured them there weren't any they were quite crestfallen and in some cases, openly sceptical.

After a few hours she was heartily sick of all the good-natured veiled, and not so veiled innuendo.

'Why?' she demanded, exasperated, 'does everyone automatically assume a single woman is on the look-out for a man? I'm quite happy as I am, and even if I wasn't I wouldn't have Gabriel MacAllister if he came free with teabags!'

She thought she'd finally made her point, until one of the day staff asked who was the gorgeous guy in the stupendous silver Merc? He was waiting for her! She felt as trapped as your average mouse would, with a big sleek cat purring outside her nest.

'If that hunk was waiting for me I wouldn't be wasting my time filling in forms,' her opposite number on the daytime shift had said, almost reproachfully.

'I'm behind on the paperwork; we were busy last night.'

She would have idled there longer had she not needed

to get back to Will. She caught up with her friend Meg just as she was leaving the building.

'Can I cadge a lift with you?'

'You prefer my Mini to what's on offer out there?' Meg's teasing expression faded when she saw how close to tears her friend looked. 'Of course you can have a lift, if that's what you want,' she said warmly.

She didn't even comment when Alice chose to furtively crouch down in the back seat until they'd left the hospital grounds.

'Thanks, Meg,' she said, when they drew up outside her parents' house.

'If you're thanking me for restraining my curiosity, don't. It's on hold, that's all. You look so all-in,' she said frankly, examining the pallor of Alice's face, 'that I'm not going to interrogate you until you've had a full day's sleep. But I forgot. You don't take a full day's sleep, do you?' She yawned. 'I've no idea how you do it, Ally. I need my eight hours.'

Alice shrugged. 'You get acclimatised. Besides, I do get a nap when Will has one. Remember I only do Mondays and Thursdays; it's not that bad.'

Meg wound down the window. 'If you say so, girl,' she replied sceptically. 'But if you don't mind me saying, you look like you could do with your bed right now.'

On this occasion looks didn't deceive. Alice just smiled wearily. 'See you Thursday.'

'He's asleep,' her mother said when Alice walked into the kitchen.

Alice frowned and glanced at her watch. Her son was a habitual early bird.

'He didn't sleep too much last night. He was quite fretful.'

'Oh, Mum, I'm sorry. You should have rung.'

'I would have, dear, if it had been necessary. Children get temperatures.'

'He's got a temperature?' Alice parroted in alarm. 'Where is he?'

'He's not going anywhere. Calm down, Ally, and sit down before you fall down,' her mother advised sternly, pushing a steaming mug of tea into her hand. 'Your father will give you a lift home when Will wakes.'

'Isn't he playing in that bowls tournament this morning?' Alice asked guiltily. 'I don't like to be a nuisance.'

'You're his daughter; it's your job to be a nuisance. Besides, your father is forever droning on about being obsolete. It'll do him good to feel needed.'

Alice, who had never heard her cheerful energetic parent do anything of the sort, maintained a tactful silence.

'I suppose you know your sister didn't come home last night?'

Alice hadn't known, and from her reproachful glance got the distinct impression that her mother somehow held her responsible.

'Do you know what she's doing? You realise she's far too young to get married.'

'I was only twenty myself, Mum,' Alice reminded her, taking a sip of the scalding tea. Coffee would have been better, to nudge her sluggish brain into top gear with a big caffeine injection.

'But you didn't have the prospect of a brilliant career, like Sophie,' Janet West told her daughter bluntly.

Why did the truth hurt? Alice wondered, aware that her mother would have been horrified had she known the casual statement made her daughter wince. There had been a lot of casual statements over the years. Most had taken it for granted that she would marry and provide grandchildren whilst Sophie would have a high-powered career.

She'd fulfilled parental expectations when, midway through her nurse's training, she'd fetched home a handsome young doctor. When Oliver had wanted them to get married before she'd even finished her training her parents had added their combined voices of approval to the plan. She sometimes thought it was her own deep-seated need to please her parents that had made her swallow her own nagging doubts and agree.

When it had come to providing grandchildren she hadn't been so prompt, and some of the heavy hints had really hurt. Alice had thought it was her fault and so had Oliver, although he hadn't come right out and said it. Often she'd got the impression she'd disappointed him.

Once she'd wondered out loud if he would have married her had he known she was barren. He'd been angry at the suggestion and he'd shouted a lot. It was only later that Alice realised that he'd never come right out and denied her accusation, he'd just made a lot of noise.

Ironically, when they'd discovered the problem lay with him their troubles really had started. Oliver had taken his infertility as a challenge to his masculinity. His confidence severely shaken, he'd responded aggressively. Perhaps he'd been trying to prove something when he'd taken a lover? She'd never got the opportunity to discover whether their marriage could have recovered from that final body-blow.

'I said do you think the university will let her defer for a year? And what about the scholarships…?'

'What…?' Alice tried to gather her straying thoughts. 'I think I'll just go and look in on Will, Mum.'

'Well, really, Ally. I do think you might show more interest in your own sister's future!'

Will opened his eyes when she walked into the bedroom. She brushed the sweat-slick hair back from his forehead;

the heat of his skin shocked her. He didn't have his usual smile for her today, the one that cracked her heart open. He squirmed fretfully when she peeled back the covers to pick him up.

She didn't need a medical degree. One look into his glazed feverish eyes and Alice knew that he wasn't a well boy.

'Come on, angel, let's get Grandpa to take us home and then I'll ring Uncle Peter to come and take a look at you.'

As she carried him downstairs he remained unusually compliant in her arms. Alice stifled the flurry of fear and forced herself to speak cheerfully when he began to whimper.

'Where's Dad?' she said urgently as she walked into the kitchen.

'In his potting shed. But can't it wait until he's—'

'No.'

'Well?' Alice said when Peter Craig had completed his thorough examination. 'And don't tell me I'm a neurotic mother!' she warned her husband's ex-partner darkly.

'I wouldn't dare,' the GP returned honestly. 'What can I say that you don't already know, Ally? He's feverish, but there's no sign of bacterial infection. It's probably a virus.'

'The doctors' standard response when they don't know what's wrong,' she observed sourly. She knew something was wrong, but how did you defend a mother's gut instincts to someone who only understood scientific facts.

'What can I say…? There is a nasty twenty-four-hour bug doing the rounds. All you can do for now is keep his temp down and push lots of fluids. If you need me ring and I'll come.'

Alice sighed. 'I know, Pete, and I'm grateful. It's just hard…' Swallowing a lump in her throat, Alice let her eyes return to her son, who smiled wanly back.

'You don't have to tell me, Ally, I'm a dad.' He patted her on the shoulder and snapped his case closed.

Alice curled up on the couch in the nursery that night, and kept jerking herself guiltily awake whenever she began to drowsily nod off. It was about seven a.m. when exhaustion finally overwhelmed her.

It was nine-thirty when an insistent pounding on the front door woke her. Rubbing her bleary eyes, Alice walked over to the low bed. One look at her son told her something was desperately wrong—the sound of his breathing, the colour of his skin.

'Will!' she cried shrilly, picking him up. There was no response. His little body lay heavy and limp in her arms. She hit the floor running.

Gabriel was standing with one hand braced against the porch wall and the other on the doorbell when the door was flung open.

One glance at the wild-eyed young woman with the still, dark-haired child in her arms told him something was badly wrong.

'What is it?' She looked at him as if she wasn't seeing him. 'Is he…?'

'He's breathing.'

Gabriel gave a sigh of relief. For a minute there he'd thought…

'We need to get to the hospital.' She was running past him as she spoke, towards the Mercedes parked in the driveway.

'Of course.'

Gabriel covered the distance to the City General in a remarkably short time. During the journey he'd rung ahead to tell the department of their imminent arrival.

'They want to know what is wrong. What shall I tell them?'

'Tell them…' she said, without taking her eyes from the child in her arms. 'Tell them he's two, not rouseable, and I think he has meningitis.' She'd known the instant she'd seen the ugly purple rash on Will's plump little legs.

'They're asking…?' Gabriel began gently. He'd never heard such tragedy in a voice.

'Yes, he has a rash, and no, it doesn't disappear under pressure.'

Once they were there, the well-oiled emergency machine sprang into action. Nobody disagreed with her diagnosis, and almost before they were over the emergency threshold they were pumping antibiotics into Will's limp body.

Nightmare didn't even come close to describing the next few hours; she'd never felt so helpless in her life. Half an hour later, when a white-coated figure she vaguely recognised came to speak to her, she couldn't really concentrate on what he was saying, even though she strained nerve and sinew to try and understand. Her brain was too full of fear.

'Got him here quickly…difficult diagnosis to make early on…the next twenty-four hours will be crucial…best paediatric intensive care in the this part of the country…'

Alice just nodded dumbly.

When he left her alone in the small waiting area it struck her for the first time that the doctor's sympathetic gaze had alternated between her and someone else. She wasn't alone.

'You're still here.' How long, she wondered numbly, had that been?

'I thought,' Gabriel said unemotionally, 'you might need someone to contact your family.'

'God, Mum!' She closed her eyes. 'I don't think I can cope with her right now.'

'You shouldn't be alone.'

'Sophie…? No. I'm not thinking straight. She tried desperately to concentrate her thoughts. 'Don't let Sophie come near. Not with the risk to the baby. She'll want to come,' she fretted, knowing her sister wouldn't accept the exclusion easily; Sophie doted on Will.

'Leave it to me.'

She nodded, accepting his assurance unquestioningly. 'I'm sorry, but they'll probably want to give all Will's contacts prophylactic antibiotics,' she warned him.

'Will you be all right alone for a little while?'

Alice felt a strange reluctance to let him go as she nodded.

Her father sat with her part of that first night, until Alice finally insisted that he go and rest. She wasn't alone for long.

'What are you doing here?'

'Your father didn't want you to be alone.' They were both whispering, even though Will showed no sign of waking.

He sat quietly down beside her. Alice was relieved when he didn't ask any questions. There was no How is he doing? or queries about the various tubes protruding from her son's tiny body… He looked *so* small.

It was about four a.m. when they gave her the news.

'Of course we're not out of the woods yet. We'll ventilate him for a few more hours, but we're quite optimistic…'

'He's not going to die?' Her dry, cracked voice sounded alien to her ears.

'You have a fighter there, Mrs Lynn.'

Alice began to shake, and the first tears she'd allowed herself began to fall. She turned blindly and found a convenient chest to lay her head against. Arms held her lightly as she wept. Eventually the tears subsided and she drew back.

'I'm so sorry.' She pushed her hair back from her face.

She couldn't seem to control the fine tremor in her hands at all. She felt embarrassed by this display of weakness and couldn't quite recall why Gabriel was here at her son...*their* son's bedside. Will deserved a father. He deserved one like Gabriel. Suddenly, unequivocally, she knew this.

'Why don't you go and freshen up...eat...sleep...?'

'I can't sleep!' she protested.

'You won't do him much good if you collapse.'

He had a point. 'Fine, I'll get something to eat. You'll get me if...?' Her eyes returned anxiously to the small silent figure on the white bed.

In the event the food she forced herself to chew tasted like sawdust, and the cold water she splashed on her face didn't alter the fact she looked almost ghoulish with the big purplish shadows under her eyes and her startling pallor.

The ever-present nurse twitched the tubes and pressed a button or two before writing indecipherable numbers down on the chart. With a frown she glanced at the child's shoulder, then abruptly her expression cleared.

'See how much better the rash is.'

Gabriel could see the purplish blotches on the child's lower limbs had got no worse, if not lessened over the past few hours.

'I thought for one minute that that birthmark on his shoulder was another one. Have you noticed how it's shaped just like a star?' she asked, before she vanished.

Gabriel sat there for several seconds before he got up to confirm the suspicion that rose up in his mind, gathering strength by the second. Two years old... Why hadn't he known the significance of two years old when he'd heard it?

He looked down at the small figure and wiped an unsteady hand across his own brow, where pearls of sweat glistened. The muscles in Gabriel's throat moved convulsively. Even with his small features distorted by the ugly tubes he could detect the familiar shape of the nose, the angle of the jaw, the width of the forehead.

He didn't even need to see the confirmation of the darkly pigmented mark on the child's shoulder. His hand went automatically to his own shoulder where, under his clothing, there lay an identical mark.

'What's happened?'

Gabriel tore his eyes from the boy's face—his *son's* face—and turned around. 'Nothing.' And everything. No wonder she'd fallen at his feet!

'I thought…seeing you standing there like that—' She stopped uncertainly. Gabriel looked so strange.

Alice shook her head slightly. She was reading too much into an imagined odd rigidity about his broad back and shoulders. The expression on his face was… Like a lot of people he probably just didn't like the medical hardware.

'I suppose I'm just expecting things to go wrong.' Was Will's colour better or was she just seeing what she wanted? she wondered, walking around to the opposite side of the bed. 'I can't let myself believe yet…' she explained gruffly. 'Thank you for staying.'

The irony hit him like a bullet between the eyes. She was thanking him for sharing a vigil over his critically ill son—*his* son. It sounded strange to even think it. He might have died and he would have been none the wiser!

'Dad will be back soon, and I don't suppose he will be able to stop Mum from storming the hospital for much longer. You can go.'

'When did you know that he wasn't your husband's—?' He broke off and pressed both hands to his forehead. He…the baby. Her son. 'God, I don't even know his name! *My own son.*'

CHAPTER FOUR

ONE shock too many! She should have seen it coming! The last gentle colour seeped from her cheeks whilst the buzzing in her ears welled and receded. When the black dots cleared from her vision she saw that he was waiting, statue-like, for her reply.

'William. His name is William,' she whispered faintly. 'We call him Will,' she added, in a stronger almost defiant tone. It was impossible to tell from his expression how he felt about becoming a father under such bizarre circumstances.

Part of her had known this moment was inevitable. She just hadn't wanted to acknowledge it. Perhaps in some strange way it was easier coming now. Being forced to face the brutal realities of life and death had a way of downsizing everything else.

'Hello, Will.'

Alice felt the sting of tears as Gabriel bent over the sleeping child. She hadn't known those hard predatory features could be so soft, so tender.

'I was going to tell you,' she whispered.

'When?'

Alice shook her head mutely but he wasn't looking at her.

'I have a son...' There was a deep sense of wonder and disbelief in his voice.

When Gabriel's attention returned to her there was no visible reminder of that tenderness; he was all hard suspicion and anger. Alice couldn't bring herself to blame him for this response.

'I always knew that Will wasn't Oliver's.' She was oblivious to the quietly dignified image she presented. All she was conscious of was the bitter nausea in her throat and the sick pounding against her breastbone as her heart tried to escape the confines of her tight chest.

'And that left...?' The angry irony she could take; she even felt it was justified. Thank goodness he wasn't shouting. She hated slanging matches, and loud voices made her shrivel up inside. The memory of the last months of her dying marriage was still strong.

'You.' Did he still doubt that he'd been the only one? What about his morals? The hypocrisy touched an inner core of anger and her blue eyes flashed.

'Didn't it occur to you that I might want to know I had a son?' His stunned eyes strayed to the child on the bed and his expression contorted with anguish.

'I didn't even know your name,' she reminded him. Shame brought a rush of colour to her cheeks and defiance to her voice. 'How was I supposed to explain that to Will when he was older?' Youngsters were remarkably intolerant of failings in their elders, and she wouldn't have been able to bear for him to feel ashamed of her and his origins. 'I wanted Will to think his father was special...'

Gabriel's head went back as though she'd struck him. 'And not just someone who happened to be in the right place at the right time.'

Alice gave a gasp of dismay. 'No...no...that came out all wrong,' she denied vigorously.

'On the contrary, you seem to have encapsulated the situation very succinctly. You must have thought the fates were against you when I knocked on your door,' he reflected grimly.

'Something like that,' she conceded unhappily. It was impossible to tell from his sardonic expression what he was thinking…feeling. What, she wondered, was going to happen now? What did he want of her, and, more importantly, Will?

'You thought you could hide it from me?' he asked incredulously. His glance shifted once more to the boy. *'He's me.'*

'Do you think I don't know?' she asked him, her voice husky with anguish. 'But would you have seen that if you hadn't found out?' A frown wrinkled her smooth brow. How…how did you…?'

'The birthmark on his shoulder. I have one, Greg has one, our mother—*his* grandmother—has one. Even without that I'd have known,' he told her positively.

The talk of grandmothers made her feel even more flustered. She half expected a crowd of unknown relations to walk through the door, each demanding a piece of her son. She couldn't stop herself glancing furtively towards the empty doorway. Taking a deep breath, she tried to calm her thoughts.

'Maybe you would, but you'd be surprised how many people remark on his likeness to Oliver,' she told him drily. 'They expect to see it, so they do.' A circumstance which had caused her acute discomfort over the past two years.

'So you didn't know who I was or how to contact me, but when I walked in the other day—you knew.' He took a deep breath and with a self-conscious glance at the quiet figure in the bed consciously lowered his voice further. 'Why didn't you tell me then?'

'And how would you have reacted? My sister is pregnant with your brother's child and I—her sister!—suddenly produce a ready-made son for you! What are the odds? Even I don't believe it!' She bit back the laughter that was borderline hysteria. 'And why would I put Will and myself through all that for a father who probably wouldn't even want to know him?

'Besides, there are other people involved here. My parents and Oliver's gran—she's very frail. She brought up Oliver and it nearly killed her when he had his accident. She dotes on Will. So if you're thinking of making some big public announcement—*Here's my son*, complete with a twenty-one-gun salute—forget it! I won't let you! Why should you be involved any more than a donor in a sperm bank is?'

She knew all the arguments; she'd been over them dozens of times before in her head. It was somehow harder to make them sound quite so authoritative when the audience was staring at her with dark brooding anger.

'I notice you've left out any mention of how inconvenient it would be for you to have the truth come out. The stoic little widow has a much nicer ring to it than the widow who leaps into bed with the first man she meets—imagine the raised eyebrows, not to mention the wagging tongues. And then there'll be the ones who might think you didn't even wait for him to die.'

The dark stain across his prominent cheekbones deepened as he spoke. He hardened his heart against the stricken look on her face. It seemed appropriate that she should at least squirm a little, considering she'd managed to disintegrate the very foundations of his life!

'Besides, the way I recall it my involvement was a bit more personal than artificial insemination.'

Of its own volition her glance shifted from the savagely confident gleam in his eyes to his expressively mobile lips. Throat dry and knees trembling, she began to study the bag of intravenous fluid hooked up beside the bed.

'Then perhaps we both recall a different event,' she

threw back with a studied dismissal that brought his even white teeth audibly together in a snarling smile. 'There's a lot more to being a father than copulation.'

'Save your sanctimonious little sniffs, Alice. Are you trying to tell me that anything other than sexual gratification was on your mind the night we conceived William? Couldn't you say there's more to motherhood than copulation?'

'What…? No… But that's…'

'Different?' he suggested. 'How convenient.' Gabriel suddenly froze. 'He spoke!'

'What?' she said sharply, moving closer with him to the bedside. 'Are you sure?'

'He's moving his hand…see.' He gestured towards the feeble flutter of the small hand against the sheet. 'I'll call the nurse…the doctor…'

'Yes, Gabriel.' Alice didn't want to raise her hopes too far but she couldn't prevent the adrenaline rush that pulled every nerve and sinew in her body taut.

Alice found it nothing short of miraculous how quickly a child could recover. Will looked too thin, she could count each knobbly prominence of his spine, and he was a little crankier than usual, but other than these temporary differences he was her Will. Or *their* Will, a fact Gabriel's almost constant company made her unlikely to forget. Nothing was ever going to be the same again.

'He can go home today?'

The tired-looking doctor smiled at her incredulity. 'Well, if you prefer to stay…'

'Definitely not! Nothing personal, you understand…' She could feel the silly smile on her face. 'I must ring home and tell them.'

* * *

Alice knew how small communities worked. Their visitors from the village hadn't commented on Gabriel's presence, but she knew that speculation must be rife by now. She couldn't decide if it was paranoia speaking when she felt sure that people were going to start suspecting soon—if they didn't already.

Her parents were still too relieved that Will was on the road to recovery to think about anything else. And Sophie hadn't asked why Gabriel was taking such a personal interest in Will's welfare. But she must know because on the several occasions she'd sent Greg to deputise for her during the past few days Gabriel had been there. It had seemed strange to Alice that Greg had apparently accepted his brother's presence without question—unless Gabriel had told him. Alice dismissed this disturbing idea. Greg had behaved far too naturally.

Alice had been forced to admit there might be more to Greg than first met the eye. He had gone out of his way to amuse her fractious son, and had displayed an unexpected sense of humour. The relationship between the brothers had surprised her too. There was an obvious affection between them, and, from Greg's side at least, a real respect for his elder brother.

'In a crisis,' he'd confided to her one day, 'there's no one like Gabe. When Dad's business was going under Gabe left university without a second thought. Our Gabe's quite the egghead on the quiet, and I know it was hard for him to turn his back on all the academic stuff. That's why I don't want Sophie to miss out on her chance,' he confessed with a worried sigh. 'Me—I'm not the brainy type.'

'Me neither.' They exchanged a quiet, comradely grin. Heavens, she might even end up liking the boy! 'What happened…to your father's business?'

'Oh, Gabe helped Dad pull things around, and though it

was tough going for a few years they never really looked back. Dad retired a while ago, so Gabe's the big boss now.'

'Do you mind?' She couldn't restrain her curiosity. It was a situation that might have bred a lot of jealousy and resentment. It said a lot about the two men involved that she'd seen no sign of either.

'God, no!' Greg exclaimed with a laugh. 'I'm far too lazy to try and compete with Gabe. That's the general consensus, anyhow.'

'Gabe...Gabriel says that?' she asked disapprovingly.

'No, Mum and Dad mostly. Gabe's got an embarrassing amount of confidence in me—especially considering...' His voice trailed off and his eyes slid from her before continuing with a rush. 'I got mixed up with the wrong sort of crowd...drink...drugs...but I've nothing to do with any of that stuff nowadays,' he assured her earnestly. 'Gabe, he stood by me when I was at my lowest,' he added gruffly. 'It would have killed Mum and Dad if they'd found out.'

'Does Sophie know?' Alice was shocked, but she found herself thinking better of the young man for his confession.

The young man nodded his head in mute confirmation. 'Gabe's a great guy.'

Alice couldn't rouse herself to contradict him. She nursed a sneaking suspicion he might well be right. For some reason this reflection left her feeling restless and almost angry.

Alice was packing Will's belongings in a holdall when she felt Gabriel's silent presence at her shoulder. She had a strange sixth sense about these things where he was concerned.

'He's been discharged.'

'So I've heard.'

Alice straightened up and swung around to face him. Her

hair, which needed trimming, swung in her eyes and she tucked it impatiently behind her ears.

She'd grow it for him, Gabriel decided, overcoming his inappropriate urge to let the silky strands slip through his fingers.

During his couple of hours' absence from the hospital Gabriel had changed and shaved. Looking at him, nobody would have suspected that he'd had anything less than his full eight hours' sleep for the past fortnight. He looked impeccable as usual, casual today, in jeans that clung discreetly to his lean hips and a black tee-shirt that hinted at his impressively muscled torso.

His vitality was an insult to her jaded senses. There's no justice in the world, she thought, glumly running a hand through her own wispy hair. She already regretted her quick peek in the tiny mirror in the parents' shower room that morning.

'Why did they tell—?' she began in alarm.

'A perfect stranger?' His voice was at its driest and her eyes slid uncomfortably from his. She knew this truce couldn't last much longer. It had been different when they had both shared a common objective—getting Will well. Now, Gabriel had his own objectives.

'It was a casual comment by one of the nurses to a family friend. What could be more natural? I've not been muscling in on your parental territory, if that's what's worrying you. But to be honest it hasn't felt comfortable to sit back and be excluded whilst the medics discuss my son's care with you.'

His candour had a definite ring of warning, but it was hard to gauge from his expression how far he was going to push it here and now.

'You didn't say.' She chewed her lower lip nervously.

'There were more important things to think about than

my finer feelings. I wasn't about to throw a tantrum and stamp my feet when the boy's life was at stake.'

The suggestion made her flush. He'd been quietly supportive, and sometimes she'd been glad of his strong presence at her side. It was foolish, but somehow she'd felt nothing bad could happen whilst he was there. That aura of strength he exuded seemed to enclose those around him in a protective bubble.

It would have been easy to become reliant upon him during those long worrying days and nights, but she had fought hard to retain her independence. She'd done without a male shoulder for a long time now—it wasn't an essential component in her life.

'And now…?' The summer-blue eyes levelled at him were deeply troubled, and the faint line between her straight feathery brows had become a deep groove in her smooth face.

'Are you afraid of me, or just of change—any change?' he mused thoughtfully.

'I'm not afraid of anyone. Certainly not you.' That didn't stop her wishing several times a day he'd never reappeared, but she was a realist, and she knew she'd have to make some concessions, but she wasn't going to let Will suffer to satisfy his paternal instincts.

'You really look very attractive when you get bolshy.' The severity of his expression was unexpectedly lightened by his grin.

Alice knew he was being sarcastic. Her sleep ration had been minimal for more nights than she wanted to recall, and her face hadn't seen make-up for the duration of her stay in the narrow camp bed beside Will on the noisy children's ward. Not putting too fine a point on it, she looked like a scarecrow!

'You're not expecting public recognition, are you?' The

light laugh and haughty expression had a distinct in-your-dreams flavour that brought an instant response from him.

'I'm not a fan of halfway measures.' There was an implacability about him that made her stomach muscles clench nervously. His wasn't a face that looked well acquainted with compromise.

'I've explained,' she began, dots of feverish colour appearing on her pale cheeks.

'About the family.' He dismissed them with an expressive gesture of one hand. 'Only I'm family too, and whilst I've no desire to be vindictive…' he paused politely until her derisive snort had subsided '…I'm not about to help you perpetuate your lie. No matter how convenient for you that would be…'

'I haven't lied!'

'That's a cop-out and we both know it,' he ground out scornfully. 'Not correcting people's misconceptions amounts to the same thing. What were you going to do when Will asked about his father? You must have thought about it now he's getting older. Wouldn't you have lied then? Produced some cosy smiling picture of Oliver for him?'

'I…I don't know.' It was something that had seemed a comfortingly long distance in the future.

'Can't you see there can be no halfway measures here?'

'You know nothing about being a parent!' she choked.

'And whose fault is that?'

'You want to be a father today, but who's to say the novelty won't wear off in a few weeks or months? I don't want to see Will hurt—it's him I'm thinking of…'

'Is it? Tell me, Alice, how does it benefit Will to deny him a father?

She felt cornered. 'I could tell them you're lying!' she told him wildly.

Gabriel looked unmoved by her threat. 'Ever heard of DNA testing?'

Alice's shoulders slumped and she put a hand to her mouth to still her trembling lips. 'How are we going to do this?' she asked dully, without looking at him.

'I thought getting married would simplify matters. What do you think?' He took a small pyjama top from her limp grasp and folded it neatly before placing it with the less meticulously packed garments. 'Your mouth's open.'

Her jaw snapped shut. 'Think?' she gasped hoarsely. To look at him you'd never know he was stark staring bonkers! He even sounded rational when suggesting insane things. 'I think you've lost it!'

'The only thing I've lost is my son, and I want him back, Alice.'

The implication was clear. He was willing to pay any price, even marriage! 'You can't take him from me!'

'That wouldn't be in Will's best interests,' he conceded clinically.

'And if in *your* opinion it was?' She didn't find his response exactly comforting.

Gabriel didn't reply, just lifted one expressive brow and let her draw her own conclusion. He knew she would. He might as well get some mileage from the fact she'd seemed to think he could give Attila the Hun lessons in ruthlessness.

'And I don't suppose your opinion is ever wrong?'

Gabriel's lips quivered as he thought of some of the major cock-ups he'd made over the years.

'I've had my fair share of mud on the face.'

Alice felt immediately suspicious of this display of uncharacteristic humility. She tried to imagine him putting an expensively shod foot wrong and failed miserably.

A movement on the periphery of her vision alerted her

to the fact they were no longer alone. The small figure flew straight past her and ran directly at Gabriel. The image seemed suddenly prophetic.

She watched as he swung the giggling child up high above his head. William displayed perfect confidence in the strong hands that held him aloft. When he returned to a comfortable perch against Gabriel's chest he held out a crumpled paper for Alice.

'Picture for Mummy,' he told her in his clear treble.

Mistily Alice looked admiringly at the childish daub. 'That's lovely, darling.' It was hard to speak past the emotional lump in her throat. The trauma of the last few days must have left her more vulnerable than she'd imagined. Afraid she was about to burst into tears, she turned away with a sniff.

'Let's leave Mummy to finish packing, champ. We can say goodbye to the fish. Would you like that?'

'Fish…fish…fish!'

His tactful withdrawal was purely coincidental, she decided, unwilling to construe his actions as sensitive.

Gabriel and William stopped to let a mother pushing a young girl in a wheelchair go by before heading for the playroom and the tropical fish tank that fascinated William.

The other mother watched them go with a smile. 'Your husband is so good with him,' she said admiringly. 'Mine can't stand hospitals. He says the smell makes him feel sick.' She sighed. 'We're hoping this one is a boy,' she confided, touching her swollen belly. 'Is he your only…?'

'Yes, Will's an only child,' Alice put in quickly, before turning back to her packing.

After a frenetic half-hour of excited rediscovery at home William visibly wilted.

'He's tired. I'll take him up for a nap,' Alice said, scooping up the tearful toddler.

'Good.' Gabriel was sitting in an armchair, his feet set wide apart and his hands placed palm-down against his thighs as he leant forward to watch them. The intensity of his regard made her uneasy—*he* made her uneasy. Despite making an effort to behave in a civilised manner towards him, she'd only gone along with him bringing them home to avoid a public scene. Her hostility bubbled just below the surface, though Gabriel looked remarkably relaxed.

'Tired of him already?' She threw the scornful accusation over her shoulder.

'No, just tired of your constant suspicion.' His tone was terse and exasperated. With a sigh he leaned farther back into the chair and ran a hand through his thick dark thatch of hair. 'We need some time to discuss things,' he added, in a more moderate tone.

Alice didn't like the sound of *things*. 'I'm all for laying a few ground rules.' It made her feel marginally better to pretend she was still in control.

Will was asleep almost immediately, so she had little excuse to linger. There had to be some sort of compromise that would satisfy Gabriel, she thought as she made her way slowly downstairs. A compromise that wouldn't tear apart the fabric of her life. She liked her life and she didn't want it altered.

The thought stirred the memory of Gabriel's accusation. I'm *not* scared of change, she silently denied, tossing her hair back from her face with a defiant gesture. It didn't make sense to mess with a formula that worked, and the past three years had been the most peaceful and satisfying of her life. She wasn't going to give it up without a fight!

She strode purposefully into the airy living room, her face alight with this new sense of purpose. She'd allowed herself to be intimidated by the man, that was her problem. Well, no more of that! She could play hardball too!

Alice stopped abruptly at the unexpected sight that met her eyes. Gabriel was half turned from her. He held a cardigan she'd left lying on the sofa in his hands. The pastel-coloured garment was pressed to his face.

He became aware of her presence almost straight away. He didn't behave self consciously, although the slither of darker colour across his cheekbones might have indicated discomfort. But she didn't think so—the man was so hard-faced!

'It smells the same as your pillow did in the morning.' His voice was low, but his dark eyes had a feverish intensity.

Alice gasped, a broken, ragged sound. Her wretched body reached boiling point in the space of a single breath. Her brain inconveniently retrieved a remarkably vivid image of how he'd looked when she'd crept away at dawn.

The muscled arm she'd furtively crawled out from under had still been draped over the side of the bed she'd just vacated. One leg had been above the crumpled sheet and had curled upwards, displaying the taut muscles in his powerful thigh and tight behind. The sweeping supple curve of his spine had been darkly shadowed, and the dawn light slipping through a gap in the curtains had cast a dappled pattern over the skin of his chest and belly.

In repose his profile had looked less harsh, his spiky lashes lying lustrously dark against the high sharp curve of his cheek. The fuzz of dark hair across his lean cheek and jaw had emphasised the angularity of his features.

'It was all I had left to remind me you'd been real.' He didn't take his eyes from her whilst he deliberately inhaled deeply.

'I'm sorry,' she croaked inanely.

'Why?'

Because she'd crept away like a fugitive at dawn. Because she'd not been able to deal with the consequences of the night before and face the confusion of her own feelings. She'd genuinely believed that her wanton behaviour that night had been the culmination of the previous week's turbulent events. Now she wasn't so sure. What excuse did she have this time? Her sensation-starved senses had responded like a junkie from the moment he'd reappeared on the scene.

'It wasn't very polite.'

'*Polite!* You're apologising for bad manners?' he enquired on a note of raw incredulity.

'I did think about writing a note, but I wasn't terribly sure about the...etiquette.' She gave a nervous, self-conscious laugh. 'I decided you'd be relieved if I just left.' Men didn't want their easy conquests to have anything inconvenient like names. Besides, he'd been so deeply asleep she wasn't sure she'd have been able to wake him even if she'd wanted to.

'I woke up wanting you.' His dark eyes blazed, and Alice was engulfed by a devastating wave of desire that left her feeling physically weakened. 'Relieved was the last thing I felt.' There was heavy irony in his earthy assurance. 'I've never had a woman walk out on me before.' Anger was now mingled with the desire in his eyes.

Alice's hand went to her throat; she could feel the heavy throb of the pulse at the base of her neck. Even though she had managed to tear her transfixed gaze clear she could still feel his eyes moving over her.

'I expect you reserve that privilege for yourself,' she managed with husky defiance.

'There are less insulting ways to part company with a lady.'

The jibe made her bite her lip. 'And you're always the gentleman. I'm very tired, Gabriel...' She yawned to emphasise the point, but deliberately he didn't pick up the cue.

'I'm ready for bed too.'

She glanced uncertainly at him. His words might have been ambiguous but the same couldn't be said for the smoky blaze of desire in his eyes. Her lips were dry and her throat was tight and burning.

'Isn't that a bit obvious even for you?' she jeered, despising the shaky tremor in her voice. 'I thought you wanted to discuss Will, but when you have the chance all you want to do is get me into bed.'

'I think we'll both concentrate better when that is out of the way.'

'If that's your best line in seduction...' she began angrily—though part of the anger was reserved for herself, because his vulgar confidence was justified. Her whole body was racked with need—she wanted to touch him, smell him, she couldn't concentrate, the merciless hunger was clawing in the pit of her belly. She didn't understand what it was about this man that made her feel this sensually aware. Lust was crawling all over her skin.

'Will needs a father, and from where I'm standing you need a man.'

'Will and I were getting on fine before you came along.'

'It's not weakness to admit you need something.'

'Meaning you!' Her laughter had a hollow sound.

'Actually I was talking about myself. That night was almost *too* good. I haven't wanted another woman since.'

She waited for the punchline but it never came. The only thing humorous about his enigmatic expression was the faintly self-derisive twist of his lips.

'Are you saying,' she began incredulously, 'that you haven't...?' She shook her head in disbelief.

'Why so surprised?' he mocked. 'How many lovers have you had in the past three years?'

'That's different.' She dismissed the comparison. She knew from experience what a highly-sexed man Gabriel was. It was impossible to imagine him voluntarily abstaining from sex. It wasn't as if he didn't have his choice of women. 'Are you saying you're impotent?' She was reduced to shocked immobility by the notion.

'No,' he said, in no way offended by her startled query. 'Just choosy. It's hard to believe how well we communicate in bed when you consider what hard going it is to make you understand the most basic concept verbally. If we spend enough time in bed, and make all our arguments horizontal ones, our marriage should stand a reasonably good chance of success.'

She couldn't let that pass! He was talking as if it was a foregone conclusion. 'I didn't think you were serious about your crazy marriage...I hesitate to call it a proposal...'

'You didn't strike me as woman over-concerned with the formalities. I've had some shallow liaisons in my time, but I've usually got around to exchanging names.' It was a cheap jibe, and he regretted that he'd let her needle him into it.

This pointed reminder of their original meeting made her flush deeply.

'I don't want or need a man, Gabriel, and I *never* intend to remarry.'

Her vehemence made his eyes narrow thoughtfully. 'Why? Because perfection can't be bettered...' His thoughts slid away from this repugnant thought. 'Or didn't the first time around come up to scratch?' It was a shot in the dark. He was astounded to see it find its target.

Her eyes slid from the speculation in his face. 'Nobody's marriage is perfect.' She wasn't about to parade the inadequacies of her marriage for him, of all people. 'You have to work at it.' Alice didn't need his expression to tell her she sounded priggish.

'Another illusion shattered!' he bemoaned sarcastically. 'I thought yours was a marriage made in heaven. That's the way local folklore tells it.'

Appearances had mattered to Oliver. She sometimes wondered whether if they hadn't spent so much time and energy keeping up appearances they might have stood a better chance of sorting out their problems! Even now she felt disloyal for even thinking it.

'My lawyer is making arrangements…'

'What?' Alice was bewildered by his words.

'Financial arrangements for Will,' he elaborated impatiently.

'I don't understand…'

'He's my son, Alice. I'm not a poor man…'

Then it dawned on her what he was saying. 'We don't want your money!' she exploded. 'I suppose to someone like you everything boils down to money!' she accused scornfully.

His jaw tightened and his eyes grew hard. 'What you want is irrelevant.' With cold clarity he casually brushed aside her protest. 'I'm not going to sit by and watch my son's mother forced to go out to work…'

'I'm not forced. I want to…'

'That's not what Sophie says. She says you hate leaving Will with his grandmother. She says you ring constantly to check on him. She—'

'Says entirely too much,' Alice said grimly. 'I suppose you expect your wife to be permanently pregnant and only allowed out of the kitchen on special occasions.'

'Maybe not *permanently*,' he conceded reluctantly. His mocking expression became abruptly stern. 'Don't play the equality card with me, Alice. You don't get enough sleep. You're too thin. You need to relax,' he told her authoritatively. 'Call me Neanderthal if you want to, but I think in a perfect world a woman, or a man, for that matter, should have the choice to stay at home with a baby if that is what they want, without feeling guilty or pressured. This may not be a perfect world, but I can make as near as damn it for the mother of my child.'

Too thin… Next he'll be asking to check out my dental work! It's easy to see why he's proposing to me, she thought, biting back a bubble of self-pitying anger, I'm such an irresistibly attractive package! The 'mother of *his* child' part was the most informative part of his impassioned statement. And to think for a minute back there he'd almost convinced her it was her he wanted! He wanted the baby so the mother came along as part of the package—a tiresome part from his point of view.

'If you weren't here…interrogating me,' she breathed wrathfully, 'I would be relaxing!'

'If I wasn't here you'd be thinking about me.'

Alice ground her teeth and sank weakly into a chair. She'd just love to puncture his supreme confidence.

'And I,' he continued, with a fleeting self-derisive smile, 'would be thinking about you.'

His words slid right under her guard. Swallowing hard, she fought against the sudden heat of sensual awareness that swept over her body. 'And how to steal Will from me…'

'I don't want to do that, and I'm pretty sure you know that, Alice.'

He sounded so damn reasonable she wanted to throw something at him. 'People like you,' she ground out bitterly, 'were sure the *Titanic* couldn't sink.'

He ignored the spurt of childish petulance. 'We both want what is best for Will.'

'Who made you the expert?'

The flash of something approaching pain in his face took her by surprise.

'I know I don't know about kids, but I think you'll find I'm a fast learner.'

The unexpected wave of tenderness took her completely by surprise. 'It must have been a shock,' she said huskily. 'Finding out like that.' There hadn't been the opportunity while Will was ill to discover how he actually felt about this role which had been thrust upon him.

He nodded slowly. 'You could say that.' His dark brows lifted quizzically. Her response had surprised him and it showed.

'I think under other circumstances you'd make a good dad,' she told him gruffly.

'Thank you…I think.' His lips quivered faintly. 'I intend to be a good dad under *these* circumstances, Alice.' He ignored the distressed movement of her head and reached down and took her hands in his. His grip was warm and firm. Her hands looked very small and pale in his. With a gentle tug she was on her feet. 'We will work this out. I promise.'

Mutely she gazed back up at him. If only she could let herself share his confidence.

'One of us has to retain a grip on reality, Gabriel.'

He laughed ruefully and took her face between his hands. 'God, but you're like a damned terrier. You never give up once you get an idea into your head.'

'If I'm going to be a dog couldn't it be something more glamorous…say an Afghan or a Setter?' She took one hand between the two of hers and pulled it clear of her face, even though it had felt kind of good there. 'I should go and check on Will,' she told him huskily, averting her head because she knew her inner indecision was clearly imprinted on her face.

'I'll come with you.' The question in his voice made her look up and quickly away. It was the explicit question in his eyes that made her knees grow weak and her heart pound.

'Upstairs?' She looked fixedly at the hand still pressed between hers. There was the outside possibility she was reading the subtext wrong, but the sexy rasp of his reply didn't allow for misinterpretation.

'That general direction.'

It was the things that weren't being said that made her heart beat too fast. If he went upstairs with her they wouldn't be coming down for some time—and they both knew it. Now was the time to show him the door. She'd be a fool not to. Why was she waiting?

As if I don't know. She derided her own hesitation. Shame at her own weakness flooded through her, but the hopeless desire for him was stronger—she could almost taste it—she wanted to taste him. The contradictions of what she wanted to do and what she ought to do were tearing her apart.

Despite his air of almost casual confidence, the wait for her response was tearing Gabriel apart too. He could handle rejection, though he suspected he'd always been pretty lucky in that department, and if a lady-friend had ever wanted more than he was willing to give—and he was always pretty up-front about that sort of thing—he'd walked away with a philosophical shrug. He didn't feel philosophical right now. If he had to walk away tonight it would hurt—hurt badly!

'Fine.' The excitement stirred deep in her belly as they

walked up the stairs. His hand brushed the inside of her wrist and she felt faint—this was crazy!

Gabriel felt the fine tremor and he smiled. He didn't even have to touch her to make her feel weak with lust. No woman had ever been this responsive to him. His fierce complacent smile faded. Who's crazy with lust here, pal? he asked himself with a spurt of painful honesty.

CHAPTER FIVE

GABRIEL'S dark eyes rested on the still figure of their son.

'I didn't know my father and he didn't want to know me. I'm not like him.'

Disgust throbbed in his husky voice, and Alice instinctively knew this wasn't the first time the idea had crossed his mind. The possibility obviously revolted him. The swift surge of compassion made her heart ache.

'It would kill me to think I could be a stranger to my son.' There was no mistaking his passionate sincerity.

Alice twitched the corners of the curtain to shut out a shaft of sunlight from the sleeping figure. She didn't know why she felt so emotionally moved by his words. It was Will and herself she ought to be concerned about—they were a team; she oughtn't to allow her protective instincts to get fired up over Gabriel. If there was one person in this world capable of looking out for himself it was this man.

'I know you've got to be part of Will's life,' she admitted after a moment, matching his soft tone.

He nodded as though her compliance had never been in doubt. His eyes remained on the sleeping child. Looking at his expression, Alice felt almost as if she was intruding on something private. It made her feel uncomfortable to think of Gabriel as vulnerable. She moved to the door, and with one last look over his shoulder he followed her.

'What I said before,' she said awkwardly, once the door was closed. 'It doesn't mean I'm going to fall in with your stupid plan…' She didn't want him to get the wrong idea.

'Which one would that be?' Head on one side, he watched her with quizzical enquiry.

'Marriage!' she snapped feeling an idiot even saying it. 'And just because we're going to... Just don't get the wrong idea!' she told him fiercely.

'Are you telling me I can take you to bed, but not put a ring on your finger?'

Alice grimaced. It sounded pretty blunt when he put it like that. 'I don't know why I...' Her face crumpled in confused despair. What was it about this man that made her so totally shameless? Why did one look at him send her hormones haywire and her native inhibitions into the nearest dark cupboard?

'Want me to touch you?'

Alice didn't notice that he spoke jerkily, that the tension in his body had hiked up several notches. She just knew that the picture his hoarse words drew made her bones ache with need.

'Need to put your hands on me?'

Heat flooded her upturned face. 'I don't...' Biting her lips, she lifted her slender shoulders. 'Physically I'm a push-over.' She found it hard to be candid, but it seemed the best way to go at this point. She hoped she was giving the general impression that coming to terms with searing sexual need was no big deal for her. 'But that's as far as it goes. The physical stuff passes,' she informed him pragmatically. 'You don't go around marrying someone just because you want...'

'To rip their clothes off?'

She sucked in her breath, angry that he could make a joke out of this.

'You'd think you were the only one!'

Alice was bewildered by his sudden anger. As she

watched his white-knuckled fists slowly unclenched. His anger evaporated behind a smoothly sardonic mask.

'I want you too, you know. Hell! Of course you know! I've not made any secret of it.'

He intercepted her open-mouthed look of startled surprise and by his standards looked almost self-conscious. Alice got the strong impression he regretted his outburst. She looked at the strong shapely hand he suddenly thrust out towards her.

'What…?'

'I think the time for talking is gone. Take me to bed, Alice.' His beautiful liquid eyes were fixed on her face as he made the outrageous request.

'M…me?' she stuttered. Hazily, at the back of her mind, she'd expected him to take matters into his masterful own hands. Finding the ball well and truly in her own court was unsettling.

'I don't see anyone else around.' He didn't look to check and he wasn't smiling; he looked deadly serious.

'Do you want me to throw you over my shoulder?' She couldn't laugh; her aching throat had closed over. She didn't want to have to think, she wanted to do this submerged by blind passion, but he wasn't playing the game.

One dark brow shot up and his mobile lips formed a quirky smile. 'Is that what you had in mind? I can see the possibilities,' he conceded warmly, 'but right now I just want you take my hand and show me where we'll make love.'

Make love. Not have sex, or even have great sex. It was idiotic and possibly a bit desperate to feel comforted by semantics. Her fingers closed slowly around his; they looked very pale and almost fragile in comparison. He flicked his wrists and his long fingers interlaced firmly with hers.

'This time you'll know...we'll both know it's me. I want your eyes wide open.'

She stared at him in confusion and felt his fingers tighten. Then it came to her. It was even logical in a perverse sort of way. He thought she'd been recreating feelings she'd had with Oliver. Whereas nothing in her life had prepared her for what she'd felt that night. *Everything* she'd done and felt had been new and outside her experience.

'You think I closed my eyes and thought of Oliver...?' She could tell from the flicker of distaste on his face that her interpretation was spot-on. 'Is that what all this is about? Your poor bruised ego?' She wanted it to be more than that, *much more*! Angrily she tried to twist her fingers free.

Gabriel had other ideas. 'It doesn't matter about then, just now.' His deep voice was raw with urgency.

He jerked her resisting body towards him. As she collided with his hard frame Alice felt her angry resistance splutter and fade. He didn't loosen his grip on her hand until he'd placed her fingers on the nape of his neck. His other hand roamed smoothly over the feminine curve of her hips until it settled around the firm contours of her bottom. Eyes half closed, he deliberately pulled her hips hard against him and tilted her face up towards him.

'This,' he told her huskily, 'is about hunger, not ego.'

There was certainly no denying the evidence of his raw hunger in the eyes that explored the soft contours of her face with an arrogant air of ownership. The pulsing thrust of his erection against her belly made her body writhe automatically against him. Who could wonder at the white-hot flare of male satisfaction in his gaze? Sexy wriggles couldn't be construed as rejection in any language!

Her own hunger was flaunting its presence in her painfully engorged nipples, the clawing excitement low in her belly and the hot, melting sensation between her thighs. He was right—primarily this was about need.

'My...my bedroom is there.' Sexual surrender made her voice sound weak and wispy. She nodded her head vaguely towards the ajar door behind him.

She was shaking and too far gone to try and hide the fact as she led him through the door and closed it softly behind them.

'It's daytime,' she said in a confused voice as she looked around the freshly painted familiar room.

'Had you forgotten?' He sounded amused, but there was no matching humour in his taut expression.

'Today has been confusing, disorientating. Such a lot has happened. I don't usually...go to bed in the afternoon.'

'What, not *ever*?' His whiter than white wolfish grin flashed out. 'We're not talking the first G and T of the day here, Alice. It's *never* too early in the day for fantasies.'

'I suppose you do it whenever and wherever!' she flared, wishing she'd bitten back the gauche words that invited his mockery.

'Even with the light on upon occasion,' he confessed drily.

'What are you doing?' she rapped out sharply as he got onto her bed.

Settling himself in a relaxed recumbent position, Gabriel stretched his arms above his head and looked at her tense figure poised very obviously on the point of flight.

'That depends on you. I'm yours to command—and, believe me, that's an offer I don't make every day of the week.'

Perhaps there really weren't any rules of engagement on these occasions, but did he *always* have to do the unexpected? How was a woman meant to know where she was, or for that matter where she was going?

'I suppose you think you're irresistible?' she mocked hoarsely.

Gabriel's eyes followed the pink flick of her moist tongue as it traced the outline of her dry lips. He levered himself up on one elbow and then with one smooth motion pulled the black tee-shirt over his head.

Alice heard it hit the floor at her feet but she didn't look—she *couldn't*! Her eyes were riveted on him. His sheer *maleness* hit her like a ton of bricks. He was just so incredibly good to look at—wide shoulders, flat belly, not an ounce of spare flesh to conceal the sharply defined musculature.

Some inner instinct told her that her response went way beyond looking at a perfect body. She stifled the appreciative groan of awed approval in her throat.

Mesmerised, her eyes moved over his deeply muscled torso. Even in the bleaching bright afternoon sunlight his skin was dark. Her fingertips tingled at the thought of touching him. Once the idea had got into her head she couldn't think of anything else.

'I'm getting lonely here.' His voice was undiluted seduction. It feathered lightly across her sensitised nerve-endings.

God, he thinks I'm going to be the wild child he bedded that night! The idea she had to live up to some sexy image he had was pretty intimidating.

'You might get bored if I join you.' She felt it only fair to warn him.

'I'm willing to take that risk.' He patted the bed beside him. 'Are you always this hard to seduce, Alice?'

'If I had been…'

Gabriel rolled onto his side as she knelt on the bed. 'We wouldn't have Will.'

'That's true,' she confessed huskily.

'There's nothing wrong with spontaneity, Alice. Just do what you want to.'

'I want to touch you.'

'Thank God for that,' he breathed.

He sucked in his breath sharply as she lay with one open-palmed hand provocatively on his chest. His skin was warm and smooth, and the dark curling hair was surprisingly soft.

'It's the sensible thing to do.' Nobody could be expected to work out a coherent relationship as Will's parents with all this lust getting in the way.

'I've always had a very practical turn of mind,' he confirmed hoarsely, linking his fingers behind her head and drawing her face down to his. His tongue slid between her parted lips and with a lost moan Alice collapsed on top of him.

'Gabriel!' she moaned when he paused in his plundering assault of her mouth.

'Yes, sweetheart?' he replied indistinctly. They lay side by side, panting in unison. His clever fingers were sliding the button loops of her blouse.

'You're beautiful.' There was flattering fervour in her husky tone, but Gabriel didn't appear to hear. He was looking at the gentle swell of her heaving breasts above her narrow ribcage.

His throat silently worked as he nudged the front clip of her transparent lacy bra with the side of his thumb and the rosy-peaked mounds spilled from their confinement.

The keening sound that came from his throat was almost feral as he bent over her. Alice's back arched as his lips closed around one unbearably sensitised nipple. Eyes closed, she let the incredible tide of sensation wash over her—she couldn't bear it, but she didn't want it to stop.

Her fingers moved deeply into the dark sleek thatch of hair that covered his head. When he lifted his head it was only to transfer his attentions to the other neglected stiff peak. His suckling continued to be by turns delicate and fierce. The exquisite agony of it blitzed away all traces of her self-restraint. Her hands moved greedily over his body, revelling in the warm satiny texture of his skin.

Alice's senses were heightened and stretched to the limit. She was conscious of each downy hair on her body, and the burning dampness on her skin where his tongue and lips had been recorded itself indelibly in her mind. When his lips once more captured hers she welcomed the wild possessive pressure and returned it as though her life depended on it. She wanted that ultimate erotic possession. She *needed* to surrender.

'For pity's sake *take me*!' she pleaded in agony.

Gabriel looked into her damp contorted face and savage satisfaction was stamped across his taut features. He scooped her up in one arm and rolled her beneath him. He was suspended above her, close, but not close enough to satisfy the writhing hunger in her belly.

Alice looped one leg tightly across his hips, digging her heel hard into the small of his back with the other heel pressed into the hollow behind his knee. Her fumbling fingers moved urgently over the slightly damp skin of his belly until she found the buttoned fastening.

Gabriel's body jerked violently before he deliberately lowered himself down on top of her. The brazen thrust of his constrained manhood against her made her bite down hard on her lip and whimper.

'You're bleeding.' His fascinated eyes were fixed on the pinpoints of blood on her trembling lower lip. He delicately blotted the scarlet traces with his tongue.

Alice was vibrating with need when he lifted himself from her. She felt bereft until she saw that he was ripping off his trousers. The cotton boxer shorts followed.

Her eyes filled with unexpected hot tears and her throat was so dry she couldn't swallow. He had a male beauty that could tear your heart out. Even if it hadn't quite vacated its designated position, *her* heart was acting in a strange and unusual manner. There were probably worse ways to die, she concluded dreamily.

It took Gabriel longer to strip her to the skin because he got easily sidetracked, his fingers stroking, gliding voluptuously over her damp, silkily smooth skin.

'Tell me…' His voice was close to her ear.

'What…?' Her hands moved greedily over his belly, enjoying the sharp gasp of ragged inhalation.

'How much you want me,' he coached.

His pupil boldly touched the pulsing hardness of his arousal. His instant groaning response filled her with a heady sense of female power. His response fascinated her; *he* fascinated her.

'I want you quite a lot,' she conceded huskily.

'Where do you want me quite a lot, Alice?' As he spoke he spread her legs apart to touch the silky inner aspect of her thighs. She moaned helplessly as his exploration grew more intimate, her head thrashing from side to side on the pillow.

'Inside me, Gabriel, please, *now*!' Her voice was shrill with desperation.

The torment was intolerable. She couldn't stand it any longer. She felt as though she would explode from sheer frustration.

'Like this…?'

'Oh, yes, love, *yeess*!' she gasped, as his penetration filled her and released the pent-up emotions. The tears began to spill onto her hot cheeks. She wrapped her long legs around him and pressed her hands against his hard buttocks.

'So sweet and tight for me.'

'Just for you!' she agreed fervently, taking little bites out of his neck.

He began to move then, his strong pulsing rhythm carrying Alice with him. The words she moaned and shouted had no meaning to her, and neither did his hoarse encouragement. They were both part of the whole experience—the perfect whole.

Just before her body was convulsed by the final violent contractions of fulfilment his voice, urgent and compelling, made her open her eyes.

'Look at me, Alice…that's right. I want you to see me when it happens.'

His face was a tight, contorted mask, the skin plastered tightly across the bones of his face. His eyes glittered and his bronze skin gleamed damply.

He watched it happen to her, saw her mouth open to gasp for air as the ripples of sensation spread from the deepest muscles in her belly to the tips of her extended toes. He let go then, and she felt the heat of his gushing release.

'You can't stay.'

'No?'

It made her nervous to know he was watching her as she pulled on the light robe. How naive she'd been to imagine she'd been closing a chapter sleeping with him. She hadn't stopped wanting him, he hadn't stopped confusing her—nothing had stopped. But a sinking feeling told her something else had started.

'My parents are coming for supper to see Will.'

'And my presence would cause comment?'

He sat up, beautifully and quite unselfconsciously naked. So much for catharsis, she thought gloomily. Immunity wasn't going to be that easy. An inconvenient inner voice asked if she'd ever really thought it would be. It had just been easier to rationalise jumping into bed with him if she told herself it was the best way to get him out of her system.

'At the very least,' she confirmed drily. Especially in his present state of undress.

'So my status is to remain your secret lover.' His brows drew together in a dark straight line as he considered this situation.

'We won't be doing this again.'

He sucked in his breath to share her horrified outrage and Alice watched the iron stomach muscles quiver in response. Oh, help! Why is he so deliciously gorgeous?

'Heaven forfend!' he gasped sternly.

'Don't look at me like that. Or do that thing with your eyebrows!' she added crossly. 'I'll tell my parents in my own way and my own time,' she added significantly.

'About marrying me?'

'About you being Will's father,' she corrected. 'I'm not marrying you or anyone else.'

'Definitely not anyone else.' His eyes narrowed thoughtfully. It wasn't the first time he'd wondered if he'd got it wrong, taking the deep-freeze response every time marriage came up *entirely* personally. Perhaps it was marriage itself that scared her rigid. She'd already almost confirmed that her own hadn't been the bed of roses everyone imagined, but had it been seriously unhappy?

The idea ought to have made him happy—it made it a lot less likely that she'd used him as a substitute for the husband—but perversely it had the opposite effect. What had the guy done to her? he wondered wrathfully. The villain of the piece was dead, so unless Alice told him he'd have to carry on wondering.

'You wouldn't have a say in the matter.'

Her childish response made him grin. 'Wanna bet...?' he drawled.

'Oh, pooh!' Hands on her hips, she remained determinedly unimpressed by this macho display.

For a big man he moved incredibly quickly. Off the bed in one lithe leap and across the room before she could even squeal in protest. His hands closed around her waist and he lifted her up until her face was level with his own.

'We'll make love, Alice, whenever and wherever I want.' His dark eyes glittered with arrogant confidence.

'And what about what *I* want?'

'Or whenever and wherever *you* want,' he conceded easily.

'You're an arrogant pig and I don't like heights.' Underneath the defiance she felt weak and breathless with excitement.

'Then grab hold, darling.'

Alice did so—just before he kissed her in a very masterful fashion.

'If you don't marry me,' he taunted her when she was completely breathless, 'I won't make love to you.'

She tried to treat this threat with the laughing contempt that it deserved, but her dry lips couldn't maintain the smile.

'That's...that's...blackmail!' she croaked indignantly. Inside she knew that when he was close like this, when she could smell him and feel his need, her sexual desire for him dominated every other thought.

'It's more food for thought,' he supplied helpfully, catching her lush lower lip playfully in his teeth and tugging gently. Alice moaned and felt her body grow limp. 'All you have to do is call my bluff.'

Her lips moved hungrily against his. 'And don't think I

won't!' she assured him gruffly, pushing her fingers deeply into his dark hair.

'Not now, though, hey?' he suggested throatily.

'No,' she agreed faintly, 'not now.'

'First prize!' Alice exclaimed, holding up the rosette pinned to the sponge cake. 'I'm impressed.'

'But not surprised,' the old lady beside her responded drily. 'I've won the damned thing for the past ten years. They're probably afraid I'll keel over if they pass me over,' she grumbled. 'It's all a fix,' she added in a loud voice as a group of judges went by. Their shocked expressions made her cackle cheerfully. 'Village fêtes are nests of corruption!' she yelled after them.

'Or you just might make the best cakes in town.' Alice bent over the pushchair. 'You think Granny Livvy makes the best cakes, don't you, sweetheart?' Will grinned his cherubic chocolate-stained smile at them both.

The old lady snorted. 'I don't think discrimination is my great-grandson's most distinguishing trait. I can't *believe* the amount of junk he's consumed so far this morning,' she observed critically.

'Well, you should know, Granny dear,' Alice responded with an untroubled grin, 'you gave most of it to him.'

'Grandparents are meant to spoil their grandchildren, and that goes double for great-grandparents. I warn you, Alice, don't go fussy on me. That silly mother of yours has already accused me of sabotaging his teeth. *Silly woman.*

'Where do you want to go next?' Alice asked, diplomatically changing the subject. Meetings between her mother and Olivia usually resembled open warfare, but they should be safe, she decided optimistically. Her mother was judging the pet competition, which should keep her safely out of circulation for some time yet.

'Well, actually I could do with a rest.'

'Of course,' Alice responded swiftly. Because of her robust and ascerbic tongue you tended to forget Olivia Lynn had turned eighty. The shoulder she squeezed felt incredibly fragile. 'Actually, my feet are killing me. We could have tea and scones.'

'I'd sooner eat shoe leather, my dear. Don't you know Rachel Mortimer made the scones this year—need I say more? No, I think I'd prefer the beer tent.'

Alice repressed a grin. 'Whatever you like, Olivia,' she agreed meekly.

They chose a vacant table in a corner. Alice inhaled deeply, enjoying the distinctive scent of warm grass underfoot mingled with the rich aroma of the locally brewed ale in the warm marquee. She smilingly fought her way through to the front of the makeshift bar, exchanging greetings with several friends as she did so.

She was so busy not spilling their refreshments she didn't spot the extra figure at their table until she was almost on top of him.

'I hate these plastic glasses,' Olivia bemoaned. 'He's sound asleep,' she added, nodding to the child in his pushchair.

Alice tried to disguise her panic as her eyes travelled from the large teddy seated on her son's lap to the tall figure casually seated at their table.

'I won it, shooting ducks. Don't look so disapproving, they were tin, Alice. I could do with a beer myself.' Gabriel glanced longingly at the foaming glass in her hand.

She slapped the glass down on the table. She didn't even pause to consider coincidence, not where Gabriel was concerned. He'd probably been stalking them! Being seen in public together was just what she'd wanted to avoid and he knew it! Lovers they might be, because she was weak and had no backbone—not where he was concerned anyway—but the emphasis was to remain upon the *secret* and he knew it!

'Then go get yourself some,' she hissed nastily. 'I don't know what you're doing here.'

'I'm being part of the community.'

'Huh!' In his designer shirt with his designer sunglasses tucked in the breast pocket he didn't look anything of the sort. Even on the streets of a hot Mediterranean town where the rich, famous and beautiful were ten a penny he would have attracted a lot more than a second glance. Here, where the annual village fête was one of the highlights of the social calendar, *everyone* was staring at him, and by association her—Alice didn't like being the centre of attention.

'Besides, I'm here as a representative of the company. We're going to match and double anything raised today towards the church tower appeal.'

'Buying friends as well as slumming it, Gabriel?'

'It's called public relations, Alice, and I can't take the credit; that's Greg's province.' Gabriel looked mildly amused by the fervour of her antagonism. 'And actually, I'm rather enjoying myself.'

'Lucky you!' she said, conveying the strong impression that she definitely wasn't!

Olivia laughed suddenly, and Alice subsided into her seat, belatedly recalling their curious audience. What, if anything, had he already said to Olivia? If he'd upset her… 'This is…'

'We've introduced ourselves, child.' Olivia brushed aside Alice's explanations. 'He's as good-looking as they say, isn't he?'

'He thinks so, certainly.'

'Alice, you'll embarrass Mr MacAllister!' the old lady chided as Alice flushed to the roots of her hair. She looked

Gabriel up and down consideringly. 'Though I doubt that. Don't choke, Alice, child. Being rude with impunity is one of the few plus-points of old age.'

'I'll let you know when you overstep the mark,' Gabriel assured her, not wilting beneath the eagle-eyed scrutiny.

'I just bet you will.' There was amused admiration in the old lady's wry voice.

God, she likes him, Alice thought, watching them. That's all I need!

'Does Alice always call you Mr MacAllister?' Olivia asked, her eyes flickering slyly towards Alice, who had to bite back a groan.

'Not in...' Dark eyes gleaming wickedly, he prolonged the torture.

The sweat trickled down her back. If he said in bed she'd die!

'...private. You look a little flushed, Alice. Too much sun?' he suggested, all concern. 'You should wear a sun hat.'

Her glossy brown hair was lightly sun-streaked, and because she hadn't got around to visiting the hairdresser's it had lost its neat geometric precision. Looking at her in the simple cotton sundress she wore made him feel hungry.

Alice caught a glimpse of that wolfish hunger when he lifted his eyes to meet her own angry blue glare. He grinned smugly back, as if he knew it had only taken a single heartbeat for her insides to turn into mush.

Alice was so involved in his eyes and the infinite dark, dangerous possibilities they could convey that she didn't immediately turn to see what the commotion a few yards away was.

'It's Helen Davey,' Olivia explained for Gabriel's benefit. Like most people he had automatically looked in the direction of the commotion caused by a voluptuous redhead who was weaving dangerously in between the tightly packed tables.

Alice winced as the woman's shrill laugh rang out. Like most tactful people, she hastily averted her gaze.

'Her husband walked out on her a couple of months ago,' Olivia explained, displaying no inhibitions herself about watching the redhead's progress towards them.

'Sad,' Gabriel remarked, displaying none of Olivia's avid curiosity. He turned his attention back to Alice, who was looking pale.

'I'm surprised he didn't do it years ago,' came the forthright reply. 'Don't you think so, Ally?'

'I really don't know.' Aware of Gabriel's hard scrutiny, she bent forward to pick up a toy that had tumbled from the pushchair. The loud voice was getting much closer.

'Nonsense, you must have seen how ill-suited they were. Alan Davey was a partner in Oliver's practice a while back. Years older than her. What job did he go to? I said—Alice...Alice!' Olivia clicked her tongue in exasperation. 'What is she doing under that table? Or shouldn't I ask?'

Alice heard Gabriel's sharp bark of surprised laughter as, cheeks flaming, she shot upright as if she'd been shot.

'He went to work for a pharmaceutical firm, I believe. A very well-paid job,' she explained with quiet dignity. I will not look at him!

'That's brought the colour back to your cheeks,' Gabriel murmured approvingly.

Her scrupulous avoidance of looking in Gabriel's direction brought her unexpectedly face to face with Helen Davey.'

'What do ya think you're looking at?' the woman slurred antagonistically.

'Hello, Helen, it's been a long time.'

'Mrs hoity-toity Lynn. Let me tell you,' she said, her

raised glass embracing the whole room, 'I could tell you a few things about the precious Mrs Lynn…' She patted the side of her nose in a conspiratorial fashion.

'Would you like a seat, Mrs Davey?' Olivia's crisp, cultured tone cut through the other woman's rambling words.

'I wouldn't take anything off you lot! Look at her, sitting there like butter wouldn't melt!' she jeered, poking a finger in Alice's direction. Her wandering gaze lighted on the sleeping baby. 'It makes me *sick* when I hear people saying how tragic it was Ollie never got to see his son.' She laughed, an ugly sound, and Alice gripped the edge of the table, knowing what was coming next. 'You know why?' She shook off a restraining hand. ''Cos he couldn't have kids. He was shooting blanks. And you know how I know? Cos he told me…in *bed.* Didn't know that, did you, Ally?' she jeered, poking her leering face closer to Alice.

Looking into the unhappy bloodshot eyes, Alice felt her instinctive revulsion followed swiftly by an unexpected surge of pity.

'Actually, Oliver told me,' Alice said quietly.

The other woman reeled back, shocked. 'He told you about me? He told you he loved me…he was leaving you…?' The plea in her voice was pathetically eager.

Alice swallowed. The woman she'd loathed for so long reminded her sadly of an ill-treated puppy who expected to be abused but still came back hoping for a kind word. She tried to cling onto her hate, but it was slipping away.

'Yes, that's right.'

Helen crumbled. Her painfully embarrassed companions led off the weeping woman.

'Olivia.' To Alice's relief, the old lady was showing no sign of imminent collapse. 'I'm sorry.' There was nothing much she could say to lessen the shock now.

'My dear girl, I've always known Will wasn't Oliver's,' Olivia told her gently.

Alice stared at her in wide-eyed shock. *'You knew?'* she echoed stupidly.

'He told me when he found out he was sterile. Though he chose to forget he'd told me. He was very drunk at the time,' she recalled. 'I didn't know about her, though.' Her thin, age-puckered lips quivered, and Alice could see the disillusioned hurt she'd wanted to protect her from in her weary eyes. 'Was she the only one?' she asked bluntly.

'I…I think so.' Alice was still too stunned to dissemble. All this time when she'd been trying to protect the old lady she'd known. 'Why…why didn't you say?' she stuttered in bewilderment.

'To what purpose? As far as I'm concerned you're my granddaughter-in-law and Will is my great-grandson, and I'll have word with anyone who says otherwise!' she warned grimly. She turned to glare at a silent Gabriel. 'And I suppose you're the father?'

CHAPTER SIX

'HE DIDN'T know!' Alice rushed in before Gabriel had an opportunity to reply. 'He couldn't...' She stopped when Gabriel's fingers closed around her wrist.

'It's all right, Alice.'

The warmth in his eyes filled her head with fresh confusion. Oh, my God! she thought in revulsion. He's sorry for me—the deserted wife. She couldn't stand pity—not from Gabriel.

'Yes, I'm William's father.' You couldn't mistake the pride in his voice. Scanning his face, Alice felt a solid lump of emotion swell in her throat.

'You didn't try and wheedle out of it. That's something, I suppose,' Olivia conceded with a sniff. 'Are you married?' Her sharp eyes went to his naked hand.

'Not yet.'

A choking sound emerged from Alice's throat, but neither of her companions let the fact she was dying of humiliation stop them.

'You know, of course, that even without that unfortunate woman's contribution tongues were bound to start wagging soon. Once you look, the likeness is startling.'

Gabriel looked towards Alice; she still looked in shock. He wondered if she realised how spontaneously she'd leapt to his defence.

'I've no objection to people knowing, and Alice's main concern was hurting you. Wasn't it, darling...?'

Darling! It fairly dripped intimacy. The look she gave him ought to have frozen the marrow in his bones, but he smiled back with a gentle understanding that made her want to hit him, and she wasn't a violent person. But then she was a lot of things with Gabriel MacAllister that she wasn't with anyone else!

'This is a very difficult situation,' she admitted stiffly.

'Depends on how you handle it,' Olivia mused.

'We'll be getting married.'

'The best solution all round,' Olivia agreed, rewarding Gabriel with one of her rare approving nods.

'Pardon me for interrupting,' Alice cut in, looking from one to the other with withering disbelief. 'Only I do have some say in the matter. I'm not marrying anyone—not now, not ever!' she declared, forcibly enough for people two tables away to turn around and stare.

'Aren't you being just the tiniest bit selfish, Alice?'

Alice stared at the old lady in disbelief. *'Selfish!'* she croaked.

'What about William?' the old lady persisted.

Gabriel's expression had a teeth-grating I-told-you-so quality. Suddenly Alice was the unreasonable one. She'd been prepared for Olivia's shock, condemnation, possibly, but the idea that she might approve of Gabriel and positively welcome the idea of them marrying had never crossed her mind.

'There you are!'

'Mother!' Alice exclaimed, relieved at this timely intervention.

'I don't know why you sound so surprised to see me.' Janet West gave her daughter a frowning look of enquiry. 'Have you been drinking beer?' she exclaimed with distaste, glancing at the almost full glass beside Alice. 'You really shouldn't; you know you've no head for alcohol. Hello, Olivia, I thought you'd have gone home by now. And how is my big boy?' she crooned.

'I'm very well thank you, Mrs. West.'

'What…? Oh…' Janet gave an uncharacteristically schoolgirlish giggle and straightened up from the pushchair and the sleeping child. 'Hello, Mr MacAllister…'

'Gabe, please.'

Alice watched with cynical amusement as he turned on the charm full blast. No wonder her mum was twittering.

'I haven't had the opportunity to thank you for being so kind when William was ill. Tom and I are both very grateful. You've no idea what a terrible time it's been for the family, and poor Sophie took her ban from the hospital very hard. She's always been a very sensitive girl, you know…'

'I was happy to be able to help a little,' Gabriel cut in quietly. 'But I'm afraid it was Alice who took the full brunt.'

'Ally has always been very capable,' Janet agreed complacently, patting her daughter's hand lightly. 'She's the practical one. An imagination,' she bemoaned, 'is a curse on occasions like that,' she told her silent daughter authoritatively.

'I've always found Ally *very* imaginative.' Gabriel's voice was at its most bland.

Alice's reproachful agonised stare was wasted on him. She got up, sat down, and got up again. She could feel the colour sizzling in her cheeks.

'Really?' Janet looked startled by this comment. 'Will you decide what you're doing, Ally?' she asked her twitchy daughter.

'I'm going…' Alice began getting once more to her feet. She couldn't take any more of this, especially as she didn't know what Gabriel was going to say next. There had been enough revelations for one day.

Three pairs of eyes swivelled expectantly towards her.

'To the loo,' she finished lamely.

'There's a queue,' her mother warned. 'It's the same every year,' she told Gabriel. 'They make inadequate provisions,' she explained delicately.

'Then why don't I take you home, Alice?' he suggested smoothly.

'Yes, do. Ally, you look washed out.'

Gabriel got to his feet and stood politely behind Alice's chair. He bent forward and looked her directly in the eyes. 'Tired, but beautiful,' he corrected firmly.

Janet's startled look gave Olivia almost as much enjoyment as the knowledge that she was privy to something the younger woman was not. Janet would hate it that she'd known first, and Olivia had every intention that she would find out.

Alice felt herself melting as she returned Gabe's warm caressing gaze; she was helpless to stop the reaction that turned her into a picture of wide-eyed, brainless adoration.

It's only a look. Anyone would think I was...*God!* What a time to realise the obvious. I'm in love with him—*how stupid is that?*

Her mind swiftly replayed some important incidents, and now she could no longer put her behaviour solely down to physical infatuation. They all confirmed this awful truth. Though she could see that from his point of view it would be convenient. Wild-eyed with panic, Alice made a silent vow that he would never find out.

'Yes, run along, Alice. Your mother will take me home.'

'What? Oh...' Janet West tore her speculative glance from her daughter and the tall young man beside her. 'I'm waiting for Tom to pick me up.'

'Excellent. I'll keep you company. That's all settled, then. Run along, children.'

Alice watched as Gabriel kissed Olivia on both cheeks, turned his thousand-volt smile on her mother and took charge of the pushchair, which he manoeuvred through the crowded marquee like a pro.

'Well! What are you waiting for?' Olivia barked. 'Catch the man! There aren't all that many worth catching these days.'

Janet West shook her head with feeling. For once the two women were in total accord.

Trying to gather her scattered thoughts, Alice did as they bid—what choice did she have? Even if they did make it sound as though she was stalking the wretched man! It was either that or watch her only child being virtually kidnapped by a stranger. Well, not quite stranger, she conceded grudgingly as she caught up with father and son.

'You behaved quite abominably in there!' she ranted self-righteously.

'You don't know restraint when you see it, woman.'

'Restraint!' she gasped wrathfully. 'My mother isn't stupid, you know.'

'No,' he conceded, stopping to let the last stragglers in a long line of small boy scouts go past. 'She's not that...'

'Why do I get the impression there's more pearls of wisdom to follow? Spit it out! You might as well make my day complete by rubbishing my family.'

'Does she always treat you like that?'

Alice didn't pretend not to understand him. 'It's just her way,' she grunted defensively. 'She doesn't mean—'

'To behave as if you're the supporting act?' His clipped voice held a hard disapproving quality.

One dark brow shot up quizzically as she gave a self-conscious shrug. Her eyes drifted uncomfortably away from his interrogative stare.

'*Sophie's* feelings...*Sophie's* sensitivity. She seemed to forget the fact you're Will's mother.' His eyes shifted briefly towards the sleeping child. 'That you carried him for nine months. At least, I'm assuming…' He looked at her in startled query as it struck him forcibly just how little he actually knew about a situation he had helped create. 'You did, didn't you? There weren't any complications?'

She had no intention of telling him about that scare early on; it was something she tried not to remember herself.

'No. My labour was long,' she recalled quietly, 'but straightforward.' Talking to Gabriel MacAllister about childbirth was second only in the bizarre stakes to seeing him pushing a buggy with panache.

'When you say *long*…?'

His persistent curiosity made her frown in puzzlement. He couldn't be genuinely interested. 'Twenty-four hours or so.'

He inhaled sharply, his eyes widening. Straightforward, she'd said! His knowledge of childbirth was sketchy, but he knew about the pain part. The thought of her going through that all alone, or at least without him, twisted his guts into knots. You shouldn't have assumed she was on the pill. He *should* have known. He should have at least admitted the possibility he'd impregnated her. He'd had the cheek to read Greg the Riot Act—at least he knew the name of his baby's mother. At least he'd be around when she needed him!

'I think we're in these people's way, Gabriel,' she said, tugging his arm pointedly when he didn't appear to hear her. She smiled apologetically at the family who were trying to move past Gabriel's immobile figure.

'Sorry.' He slickly pulled the pushchair to one side. 'You weren't…alone?' he asked hoarsely.

'Well, Mum did stay for a while, but she got too upset to stay.' It had apparently brought back too many bad memories from her own traumatic deliveries.

'I'm sure when Sophie delivers she'll elbow Greg out of the front row.'

Alice didn't respond, because she knew this acid observation was very probably correct.

'Never mind. Next time you won't be alone.' He set off at a cracking pace towards the colourful sea of cars parked on a field adjacent to the church and village green. A white dancing heat haze rose from the collective hot metal.

Alice caught up with him as he reached his car. *'Not alone!'* she squeaked breathlessly. *'Next time!'* Her voice rose a quavering octave. She angrily hooked the shoestring strap that had slipped over the curve of her shoulder back into place. Her lightly tanned skin was tingling where his dark eyes had warmly lingered.

Gabriel's grin acknowledged the fact he'd been staring without in any way offering an apology for the fact.

'Yeah,' he announced casually. 'I've been thinking it might be a good thing if Will had a little brother or sister.'

Alice planted her hands on her hips and looked at him in open-mouthed incredulity. '*You* think?'

'Naturally we'll discuss the matter.'

'That's very considerate of you,' she drawled sarcastically.

'It's the way I was brought up,' he admitted modestly.

'I just hope your insanity isn't genetic, for Will's sake. Is this…*this* supposed to happen before or after our fictional marriage?'

'I'm an old-fashioned sort of guy,' he conceded.

'Certifiable, more like!'

'I'll take that as a definite maybe, shall I?'

Alice snorted. She felt the sweat trickle slowly down her back. She'd had a more reasonable conversation with a brick wall. Her head was throbbing fit to burst from the traumas of the last hour. I can't be in love. I *won't* be in love, she thought defiantly! Looking at his handsome face, she suddenly knew how futile such bravado was.

'That's right—you think about it. I'm sure you'll find it's the most logical step to take.'

'I'm not logical!' she shrieked. If she had been she'd never have fallen for such an infuriating man!

'I'd noticed that,' he agreed regretfully. 'You had one bad experience; don't let that put you off marriage. It has its good points.'

She could hardly defend her marriage in light of recent revelations. 'In that case why haven't you ever sampled its delights?' Head flung back, hands on her hips, she gazed derisively up at him.

'I've just been lucky, I guess…' One dark brow rose to a satirical angle. 'What do you want me to say, Alice?' he appealed wryly. 'Sure, I've had a couple of near misses—what you'd term narrow escapes, I suppose… I've met some cynics in my time, lover, but you take the biscuit.'

The way his tongue curled caressingly around the word 'lover' made her stomach muscles quiver. 'I'm not cynical, just realistic,' she told him gruffly. 'Marriage is meant to be a partnership…'

'So…?' His broad shoulders lifted.

'So there's no such thing. Equality only exists on paper,' she told him hotly. 'Someone always dominates in any relationship and the other one ends up compromising.' She stopped, appalled at how revealing her corrosive comments were to anyone with half a brain—and unfortunately Gabriel's intellectual capacity had never been in doubt.

'You can dominate me any time the urge takes you, Alice. I'm pretty adaptable in that direction.' His dark glance moved lazily over her angry face and the expression in the liquid depths was overtly sexual.

Her stomach muscles spasmed this time, and sexual desire as hot as it was unwanted swept over her. That he could reduce her to a quivering collection of erotic cravings so easily was terrifying.

'Do you always have to reduce everything to its lowest common denominator?' she rasped hoarsely.

'Just because you enjoy surrendering control sexually—because there are moments when you get ultimate pleasure from being dominated in the bedroom—doesn't translate into slavery in other aspects of life. That's plain crazy. We're not talking subjugation here, we're talking freedom—freedom to express yourself sexually.'

A choking sound emerged from Alice's throat as she fought frantically to clear the occlusion there. 'How can you be so…so…coarse?' she managed eventually. Right out here where anyone could hear too!

'Do you see me bleating because you have more power over me in the bedroom than any other female on the planet!'

'I do?' she gasped. Then quickly, in the vain hope he hadn't noticed how gratified she'd sounded, she rushed on. 'I never bleat!'

'You do purr sometimes, though,' he reflected warmly. 'I don't feel I've lost my identity because I wake up in the night wanting you.' No, just my mind, he reflected wryly.

'Will you stop talking to me like this?' she hissed, throwing a helpless look over her shoulder.

'Yeah, it's hell getting turned on when you can't do anything about it,' he agreed sympathetically.

'I am not turned on!' she yelled.

'Morning, Vicar!' Gabriel nodded cheerfully at a point over her shoulder.

Scarlet-cheeked, Alice spun round only to see empty space.

Licking his forefinger, he chalked up an invisible point in the air. 'Got you!'

Alice audibly ground her teeth and glared at him with loathing. 'Anyhow, I can't get into the car with Will.' At least there was no way he could get around this one—not while he was playing the concerned father, she thought, finding comfort in this very small prospective victory. 'You don't have a baby seat.'

'As a matter of fact I do.' He swung open the back door of the car to reveal a brand-new baby restraint.

Alice tried and failed to detect a hint of smugness in his face. He could afford to be generous in victory, she decided glumly.

Will didn't wake as his father carefully transferred him to the car.

The journey home was completed in total silence—a circumstance Gabriel didn't comment on until they'd both got out of the car.

'It's all right, I've got him,' Gabriel said, scooping up the sleepy child before she could.

'Over my dead body,' she muttered under her breath.

'I didn't know you were a sulker.' He inclined his head towards the now empty car. 'The silent treatment.'

'As you don't listen to a thing I say, I don't see much point talking to you.'

There was no trace of the taunting mockery in his face as he caught hold of her shoulder with his free hand. 'It's you that isn't listening,' he told her harshly. His eyes touched the tousled head that rested on his shoulder. 'I want my son, Alice.'

His expression left no room for doubt that he meant every syllable of this simple statement. Alice felt the prickle of hot unshed tears behind her eyelids.

'And where do I come into this equation?' She bit her lips, immediately wishing the question unsaid. It was too close to a plea for comfort.

'There's nothing ambiguous about a proposal of marriage. It's not something I've done before.'

'Not even with your near misses?'

Amusement lightened the severity of Gabriel's expression and she blushed rosily. He probably thought she was fishing for some insincere compliment. *I've never been in love before!* would have been nice—unrealistic, but nice.

If you want to retain a little dignity, Alice, keep those fantasies under control!

'Possibly "near misses" was a bit of an overstatement,' he confessed.

'Spare me the details,' she begged.

'Perhaps we should go inside to continue this discussion,' he suggested gently, touching her shoulder.

Alice made coffee and he put Will to bed—as though, she thought, watching him climb the stairs, he's always been part of our lives. She couldn't let herself think that way; it would be so easy to accept what he was offering.

'I've switched off the phone.'

Gabriel set aside his coffee and, chin resting on his steepled fingers, watched as she took a deep steadying breath and began to nervously chew a strand of glossy brown hair.

'To give me your undivided attention?' The possibility was more pleasurable than he'd have dreamt possible a few weeks ago.

'To avoid talking to my mother.' She frowningly dashed his hopes. 'She and the whole village probably know about you...us by now. The grapevine is a very sophisticated form of communication hereabouts,' she told him, her voice tinged with a degree of bitterness. 'At least there won't be any need for a public announcement.'

'I'm glad to see you're the sort of girl who looks for the silver lining.'

Alice chose to ignore this piece of obvious irony.

'No more secret lover...?'

His darkly textured tone made her stomach muscles quiver helplessly. There was something almost mesmeric about his dark eyes as they rested fractionally too long on the trembling outline of her soft lips.

'I almost regret the passing of our short-lived clandestine relationship. But don't worry,' he told her cheerfully, 'I'll think of something to keep things spiced up.'

'You make it sound,' she spluttered crossly, 'as though we had some sort of formal arrangement, not a...a...'

'An irresistible attraction?'

The thought that Gabriel found her irresistible was a very attractive one. 'You don't have to talk like that. I know you only want to marry me because of Will.'

'The great sex never crossed my mind,' he agreed solemnly.

'We'll work something out so that you can have access to Will.' She knew she was babbling but she couldn't seem to slow down. 'Anyone can see you care about him,' she admitted awkwardly. 'Marriage is a rather dramatic way to prove you're a caring father, besides being rather unnecessary in this day and age.'

It was tough going, but she actually managed to keep her laughter light and her smile low-key. 'I really must make it clear once and for all that I've no interest in marrying you—even for Will's sake. I hope this will put an end to any more foolish talk.'

Gabriel didn't appear overly impressed by her mature,

reasonable attitude. I'd have got just as far screaming and shouting, she thought in weary exasperation.

'Once bitten...?'

Alice found his grim speculation cruel, and her eyes shone with angry reproach as she rounded on him. Wasn't he satisfied with the dirt he already had on her marriage after this afternoon? She was a very private person, and it made her shudder every time she replayed that awful sordid scene in her head.

'Well, if I couldn't make a marriage that began for all the right reasons work,' she challenged hotly, 'what chance would we have?'

Gabriel visibly flinched, and she stifled a surge of remorse. Small wonder he was taking it harder than you'd expect. The man just had zero experience dealing with rejection! She had to make him recognise the inescapable logic of this.

'And what exactly are the right reasons? Love...?' The corner of his mouth lifted in a fastidious sneer. His dark eyes didn't leave her face for an instant.

'I loved Oliver.' His sneer grew more pronounced, but she ploughed on, regardless of his scorn. 'And he loved me when we got married. But I'm not sure how much love there was by the time he died.'

'He wasn't going to leave you for the redhead in the bar, was he?'

'Probably not,' she admitted slowly. 'Oliver said not.' But she'd stopped setting much store by what Oliver said long before she knew about his affair and it showed clearly in her voice.

'Then why...?'

'Because there was no point hurting her, was there?' she snapped back. She couldn't shake the nasty suspicion that

Oliver's death had hurt his mistress more than it had herself. What did that say about her?

'I'd have thought,' Gabriel began, his eyes scanning her flushed face, 'that you'd have wanted to put the boot in.'

'Oh, I'm as vindictive as the next person.'

Gabriel found himself doubting that, but kept silent.

'When I did want to…how did you so prettily phrase it?…put the boot in, I couldn't do so without running the risk of telling the world what had been going on. Appearances matter, you know…' There was bitterness in her voice as she tried unsuccessfully to rub away the tight feeling in her temples.

'I hear he'd been drinking when he wrapped himself around the lamppost.' Gabriel watched her go paper-white and a nerve in his jaw twitched.

'You didn't just *hear* anything,' she fired back angrily. 'That's not the sort of information that people casually volunteer. You must have been digging.'

His broad shoulders lifted in acknowledgement as he got to his feet. 'Information is power.' He sounded outrageously casual about this ruthless viewpoint.

'Not over me, it isn't.'

'Is that what you think marriage is about, Alice, power?'

She found the unexpected gleam of sympathy in his eyes more difficult to take than his scorn.

'Did he always play around?'

'No, and it wasn't really his fault.'

'You're defending him!'

His incredulous bellow made her wince.

'A man doesn't look elsewhere if he's getting what he needs at home.'

'Did *he* say that?'

'Not in so many words, but you can be sure my mother will,' she predicted wryly. 'Oliver…we always wanted a family, and we assumed that it was my fault nothing happened. When Oliver discovered he was sterile he…he found it difficult to deal with… He was actually torn apart with guilt the night he told me. He wanted a fresh start…' Her voice faded as she was transported back in time to that fateful night. 'I was angry. I wouldn't forgive him. I said a lot of awful things to him.'

'How terrible of you!'

Alice looked up, startled by the savage mockery in his tone.

'The guy wanted absolution and you weren't playing the game.' Gabriel's crisp voice unemotionally summarised the situation she'd described. Inside he didn't feel unemotional; he was filled with frustrated rage at the irresponsible idiot who had emotionally scarred this woman. He had to bite his tongue to stop himself pointing out the strong possibility that it was a mercy he hadn't killed some other poor innocent along with himself—the selfish bastard! 'He went off in a huff and killed himself. You weren't responsible, except in your own mind.'

'How…how did you know…?' she gasped brokenly.

He caught hold of her chin and looked into her sweetly familiar face. 'I know you.' His confidence was profound.

'How can you…?'

'I know you were responding to *me* that first night, not a memory.' The heavy pause was just long enough for her to deny it.

How could she deny it? Even though he seemed perilously close to the truth.

'And I know you ask too many questions. But I can fix that.' He did.

The toe-curling kiss sizzled away any last shreds of resistance. By the time a few steamy moments had passed the only question on Alice's mind was how long she could stand the sort of torture his searing kisses and clever caresses were inflicting on her aching body. When he picked her up in his arms as though she weighed no more than a child she gave a voluptuous sigh of anticipation.

'Where are you taking me?'

The skin was stretched tightly over his high slanting cheekbones along which a dark flush ran. 'Bed.'

For once Alice didn't feel the need to question his decision.

It was two in the morning when the phone rang. Alice was too befuddled with sleep to prevent Gabriel from picking up the receiver.

She held out her hand but he didn't hand it over. Does the world and his neighbour know he stayed the night? she wondered, not feeling nearly as concerned about this as she ought. If Gabriel was trying to wear down her resistance he was doing a good job of it, she admitted wryly to herself. She still didn't know at what point she had accepted he was staying the night. He seemed to be very skilled and worryingly sneaky at infiltrating himself into her life.

The conversation seemed to consist almost completely of terse, monosyllabic questions on Gabriel's part. He was raised on one elbow and turned half away from her. She couldn't see his face but she did have an excellent view of his impressive back and shoulders. She stifled a tiny sigh of appreciation as she watched the tightly packed muscles and sinew gliding beneath the satiny smoothness of his tanned skin.

She didn't know anything was wrong until he hung up and rolled over to face her.

'What...what is it...?' The sour metallic taste of fear rose in her throat as she met his grave eyes.

'It was Greg. He's at the hospital...'

'Sophie?' she asked sharply.

'A problem with the baby,' he confirmed quietly.

'Has she…?' She couldn't bring herself to ask the question. It all came rushing back—the long weeks spent in hospital, not knowing whether she was going to lose the baby. She hadn't really known until then how much she really wanted that baby—wanted William. She still felt ashamed when she recalled her earlier ambivalence.

For a second he thought she was going to faint, but as he watched she visibly controlled her reaction. 'They don't know yet.' His dark eyes were filled with compassion. 'She's asking for you.'

Alice flung back the bedclothes, oblivious to the fact the weak rays of moonlight shining through the open curtains gave her slim body an opalescent sheen. He watched as she started pulling items haphazardly from a drawer.

She had a black sleeveless turtleneck half over her head when she suddenly remembered. 'Will! What am I going to do? Sophie needs me!' Her face, emerging from the knitted cotton, was filled with worried conflict. She'd just have to wake him. The prospect of dragging a sleepy two-year-old to a hospital in the middle of the night was not pleasant.

'Don't worry about Will. I'm here.'

'You don't mind staying?' Relief surged through her.

'There's no way you should drive right now—a taxi's on its way.'

'It is?'

'I'd like to take the credit,' he admitted as she gazed at him with undisguised admiration, 'but it was Greg's idea. He's got his hands full right now, so I offered to contact your parents and tell them what's happened. Hopefully your dad will stay here with Will whilst I bring your mother along to the hospital.'

Alice's watery grin was grateful. 'I'm sure Dad will be

only too happy to stay out of the way here,' she told him drily. 'Do you know what you're letting yourself in for? Mum will be…'

'I'll cope. And don't fret—I'll also resist any temptation to administer the traditional remedy for hysteria.'

She hadn't paused to put a bra on under the tight top and Gabriel felt his eyes drawn once more to the firm rounded outline of her delicious breasts. A sudden rush of dark colour accentuated the high slanted angle of his cheekbones. It had to be borderline indecent to be so physically conscious of her now, at a moment like this.

There was something steadying in his firm voice that enabled Alice to claw her way back from the brink of panic. She'd not do Sophie any good by becoming hysterical.

'Thank you.' There was a husky catch in her voice.

Her eyes brimmed with misty gratitude as she spontaneously reached up and kissed his lean cheek—it was a chaste salute which substituted warmth and friendship for lust. In some strange way she'd never felt this close to him before.

When she pulled back Gabriel looked the nearest to disconcerted she'd ever seen him. His hand moved to loosen the invisible tie at his throat, and then self-consciously fell away as he realised he wasn't just not wearing a shirt—he wasn't wearing anything. He cleared his throat noisily.

'It's all part of my evil plan to make myself indispensable.'

Alice extended her hand and her fingers grazed the side of his stubble-roughened jaw.

'It's working,' she told him gruffly. She saw his eyes widen suddenly with surprise. He stretched out his hand towards her and Alice took a fearful step backwards—she wasn't ready. Not yet.

'I'll just look in on Will.'

She'd been paranoid about him since they'd come home from hospital, checking on him several times a night, but for once it wasn't maternal concern which sent her towards the nursery; it was an inner conviction that if she stayed in that room much longer she'd say something irretrievably stupid—if she already hadn't!

Leaving their mother occupying the seat Greg had vacated for her at the bedside, Alice slipped quietly from the room, trying not to disturb her sleeping sister. She reflected that the anaesthetic-induced drowsiness was probably a blessing under the circumstances.

Alice had felt frustratingly impotent when faced with the misery in her sister's shadowed eyes. Her words of comfort had emerged as trite hackneyed platitudes.

It could have been me! Alice was lost in her dark thoughts when she heard him. And she was astounded at the flood of relief that surged through her at the sound of Gabriel's deep voice. Unconsciously her stride lengthened as she hurried towards the plush seating area in the foyer of the brand-new maternity wing. This place had no memories for her—Will had been born in the old Victorian building which was due to be demolished.

'I *know* you're not going to fall to pieces, man…'

Alice paused, unwilling to intrude on the fraternal tête-à-tête.

'I wish I felt as confident.' Alice felt sympathy as she heard Greg's sharp self-derisive laugh. 'I couldn't do a bloody thing!' he continued.

'You could *be* there, and you were.'

'I know I was scared when I first knew, Gabe, but…I really wanted this kid!'

His voice cracked and Alice drew back farther into the shadow of a bank of tall greenery. She swallowed the emotional boulder which had developed in her throat. Other than the sound of what might have been masculine hugs and shoulder-patting there was silence for the space of several moments.

'Who knows? In the long run this might have been for the best, Greg. She's very young—you both are. There's time enough for you both to think of families later on. A baby has never been the best reason in the world to get married. Maybe what you have will last—maybe not. This way at least neither of you are going to feel pressurised into doing something you might regret later on.'

Standing there in the humid night Alice felt icy. God! What an idiot I've been to even imagine his desire to marry me was inspired by anything other than a sense of obligation!

His advice to Greg spelt out pretty clearly how he felt. She could have wept, but she didn't—dry-eyed and stony-faced she stood stock still as all those foolish, embryonic little dreams she'd begun to spin—dreams she didn't even dare acknowledge, even privately—died.

'Well, you don't have to feel pressurised, Gabriel, because I wouldn't marry you if my life depended on it!'

Both men turned to stare at the slim, coldly composed figure who had materialised beside them. Her bleak blue gaze, scorn-laden, held his startled dark gaze for the space of a heartbeat before she turned sharply on her heel and walked away across the empty foyer.

She heard him swear, and then call her name. She didn't pause or look back, but though the deeply carpeted floor muffled the sound of his tread she sensed he was following her.

'Alice!'

She angrily jerked off the restraining hand. 'The only thing *I* regret is letting you weasel your way into my life!'

'Alice, I wasn't talking about us; I was trying to make Greg feel better. You saw him. He's wrecked over this. Admittedly I make a poor sort of Pollyanna.'

'You can make jokes while my sister is lying there feeling...*empty*.' She gave a shudder of distaste. 'I expect you think it would have been a *good thing* if I had lost Will.' A dry sob brought a raw rasp to her anguished words. 'Well, I nearly did.' She watched the colour drain from his face. 'Unfortunately for you I didn't lose my baby.' How could anyone ever think losing a baby could possibly be a *good* thing?

The air whistled through Gabriel's clenched teeth as he gasped.

Her cuttingly sarcastic shrug made no allowances for his unhealthy pallor. 'I suppose some people have all the bad luck. No Will—no need to marry his mother!'

'That's not why I want to marry you, Ally.'

Alice needed all her resolve to resist the urgent appeal in his eyes as they bored into her. 'No? I suppose you're going to wheel out the old *lurve* ticket next?' She gave a sneering laugh. 'Forget it, Gabriel, I'm not buying your lies anymore. You try very hard to disguise it, but deep down you're just like your father. You don't want a family or the responsibilities that go with it.'

If he'd been pale before, now he was grey. His expression seemed frozen in suspended animation but his eyes burned. This time when she turned to go he didn't try and prevent her.

Alice stumbled through the big glass turnstile doors, almost blinded by the tears that streamed unheeded down her face.

CHAPTER SEVEN

'I WAS nervous, but they were so lovely.' Sophie smiled beatifically at her sister and mother. 'They're really looking forward to meeting you both!' she told them happily.

Gabriel's mother and stepfather. My son's grandparents—I can hardly wait! Alice thought, pinning a bright meaningless smile on her face.

'Wasn't it marvellous of Greg to whisk me off to their villa in Tuscany?' Sophie chattered on excitedly. 'Did I say the family spend every summer there?'

Only once or twice, Alice thought drily as her cheek muscles began to ache from her expressing her pleasure. If she heard another word about the marvellous MacAllisters she'd throw up, she decided sourly.

'I didn't think it was a good idea after…' A shadow crossed Sophie's pretty face. 'But you were right, Mum, it was just what I needed.' She stared dreamily down at the brand-new diamond sparkling on her finger. 'Who'd have thought I'd end up getting engaged?'

'Not me.' Alice's response was far too spontaneous to be diplomatic.

'I always knew you two were meant to be together.' Janet West sent her elder daughter a repressive glance.

Alice conceded the warning with an apologetic shrug. She wasn't her mother's favourite person at the moment, but that silent reprimand had been earned. Anyone would think I begrudged my own sister her share of happiness. I'm obviously turning into a bitter, twisted old witch, she decided guiltily.

It was really marvellous to see Sophie had lost that awful pale haunted look. But Alice had mixed feelings about the reason—and not just on account of her sister's age. Yet another thread was drawing her into closer contact with the MacAllisters, and she was beginning to feel there was some conspiracy at work. She was definitely showing early signs of paranoia.

Who could have predicted that losing the baby would have actually drawn the young couple together? In contrast, her own tenuous relationship with Gabriel had fallen apart at the first signs of stress. Alice tried to contrast the two very different outcomes without feeling bitter. Far better to find out how weak the bond was now than later on, she decided, trying to put a positive slant on things.

If Sophie was to be believed she'd seen a new side to Greg, and Alice felt inclined to believe her. She'd come to the grudging conclusion herself that there was more to that young man than was apparent at first glance. He certainly didn't lack youthful enthusiasm. The speed with which they'd set the wheels in motion made her head spin—though the fact they seemed to be rushing into things worried her. Perhaps she was just too old and unspontaneous. Already they'd picked out a flat in Oxford, which they intended to share once the university term began. At least the wedding wasn't to be until the following summer.

'I'm glad that at least one of my children is not too cynical to appreciate the benefits of marriage.'

Alice didn't have to be psychic to know this little dig was meant for her. 'Mum,' she said tightly, 'I've told you, I don't want to discuss it.'

'It's bad enough that the whole village is talking about *it.*' Janet gave a shudder of distaste. 'I can hardly hold my head up any longer,' she told her children faintly.

'Hopefully Sophie's engagement will give the gossips something else to think about.'

Once her mother had grasped the inconceivable fact that Alice had no intention of marrying William's eligible and incredibly wealthy father—and Alice suspected that these details were the only things that had sustained Janet through the public disclosure of her daughter's depravity—she'd been determined to nag her into submission.

Though she might make light of her mother's social aspirations, Alice knew that the situation had been a genuinely traumatic one for her. A teenage pregnancy had been bad enough, but to have it made public knowledge that her only grandchild had not been conceived within the marriage bed—!

In public they had outfaced the gossips and defended both their daughters at the first hint of criticism from those only too happy to throw the first malicious stone. But Alice knew their parents had been deeply shocked by the events that had rocked their conventional world to its roots. At least Sophie was making amends now…

She just wished Mum wouldn't cling to the hope that she too would do the respectable thing. Alice had nearly told her on several occasions that as Gabriel had been conspicuous by his absence and silence since that night at the hospital it probably wouldn't do any good if she *did* change her mind—not that that was an option she'd consider!

'It's not official yet—the engagement,' Sophie reminded them. 'Not until after the party. Gabe has booked the entire hotel, you know, for guests who want to stay over.'

So it was *Gabe* now. Illogical though it might be, the casual use of his name sent a knife-thrust of…surely it wasn't jealousy? The idea made Alice wince despairingly.

Gabriel's name had cropped up every so often in Sophie's conversation, but Alice had been surprised and secretly frustrated at how sparing her sister had been with the details. It had been all she'd been able to do to prevent herself grubbing around too obviously for details—not a pretty sight! What had she expected anyhow—a private message? Hardly likely under the circumstances, she derided herself.

'The *entire* hotel? That seems a rather ostentatious gesture to me.'

Sophie gave her sister a reproachful look. 'They've got a lot of friends, Ally…'

She saw the unhappy downturn of her sister's lips, but even though she hated herself for it couldn't resist another spiteful dig. 'I've noticed that's often the way with the filthy rich.'

'I wish you could be happy for me, Ally.'

Alice leapt up from her chair, her expression contrite. 'What a nasty cow I am, Soph. Take no notice of me. I am happy for you—*really* I am. It's just a bit awkward…things being the way they are.'

'And whose fault is that?' Janet interrupted indignantly. 'We could be celebrating your engagement too. Olivia said he as good as told her he wanted to marry you. Though why,' she continued in a disgruntled tone, 'either of you should be discussing such things with *her* I don't know! She took great delight in telling me about it, you know. You have no idea how much it hurt to have strangers know before your own mother. You always were a secretive child,' she recalled bitterly.

'Olivia is hardly a stranger, Mum.'

'Olivia wasn't the only one to know before me. As for that woman—she's so hard. Do you know, she actually had the audacity to tell me that before his death Oliver's drinking had been getting out of hand for some time?' Misinterpreting Alice's shocked expression, she rushed on indignantly. 'I know, darling…' She soothingly patted Alice's arm. 'I don't know how she can talk about her own grandson like that either. Perhaps she's going senile?' she mused optimistically.

It was amazing, Alice reflected, smiling stiffly. Even learning that Oliver had been having an affair hadn't destroyed her mother's affectionately rosy view of her son-in-law. It *definitely* hadn't excused the fact her daughter had conceived a child by another man. *Two wrongs don't make a right, Alice!*

Olivia had never even hinted at the time that she shared Alice's concerns. Alice felt a surge of affection for the old lady. Knowing how much she'd cared for Oliver, she knew how much it must have hurt her to see him drinking too much, and he had been.

'He didn't drink when he was working,' she said quietly. 'Oliver never put his patients at risk.' She didn't add that she'd been constantly fearful that he might one day.

'Alice, what are you saying?'

Sophie, she noticed, didn't look as shocked as their mother, who sat there with her mouth ajar. Had she suspected…? No, she'd been much too young at the time. Maybe not too young, though. It was amazing how little youngsters missed—even Will, at his age, seemed aware that the big person he'd taken a shine to was now missing from his life. If this turns out to be a permanent state of affairs, will it be my fault? she anguished. My son will suffer because I've made his father hate me! Is nothing I do ever going to be the right thing?

'I'm saying, Mother, that Olivia was right. Oliver did drink too much.'

'Ally, he didn't…didn't get violent, did he?' Sophie's smooth brow creased as her eyes filled with tears.

One last nail in the coffin of my fairy tale marriage, Alice thought, unhappy to be the one who spoilt her sister's fantasy. Still, better she embark on her own fairy tale with her eyes wide open, she decided soberly.

'No, of course not.'

His belligerence had been loud and vocal, but never physical. When he'd been drunk her husband had seemed to hate and resent her. The worst part of it was she'd found that eventually she hadn't even been able to reciprocate his dislike. All she had been able to feel for Oliver had been a weary indifference by the end.

'He had a problem, and I'm sure he'd have dealt with it eventually.' She pretended a confidence she'd never felt; the intensely personal subject was one she didn't feel comfortable discussing.

'I think I'll just go and make a fresh pot of tea.' Janet rose hurriedly and left the room.

Alice watched her mother disappear from the room with a concerned expression. She wasn't as young as she once had been… 'I wish I hadn't told her.' Her expression was self-condemnatory. 'She adored Oliver.'

'We all adored Oliver, but I think maybe Mum adores *you* more,' Sophie responded drily. 'It's hard to suddenly discover that you didn't notice that someone you loved was miserably unhappy.' The personal note of bemused disillusionment in her sister's voice was hard to miss.

This reason for their mother's sudden departure hadn't occurred to Alice, and the surprise showed in her startled expression.

'I wasn't unhappy, *exactly*…'

'Of course not. You were blissfully ecstatic. What woman wouldn't be with a husband who slept around and drank himself to sleep?'

Alice flushed. When Sophie put it like that it made her sound like some sort of martyr for putting up with the situation for so long—she hadn't been. It was hard to explain to someone on the outside that things hadn't deteriorated overnight. The disintegration had been a gradual insidious process.

'There were good bits too,' she protested. 'And I didn't know about…'

'The other women?' Sophie gave a wry laugh. 'I used to laugh when Oliver called you a wet blanket.' She shook her head from side to side. 'He was a charmer…'

'I know, and he had a lot of good points.'

'You deserved better!' Sophie hissed forcibly.

Alice was touched by her sister's protective anger.

'Greg said I wasn't to interfere, that I shouldn't mention it.' Sophie's torn but mutinous expression showed clearly she had no intention of following this advice. 'But I think you have the right to know the truth… Not,' she added, wrinkling her brow, 'that we know what that is, exactly.'

'I've no idea what you're talking about.'

Sophie responded with a misty-eyed look of affectionate sympathy that made Alice doubt she was going to like whatever her sister felt obliged to disclose.

'You know that Gabriel turned up at the family villa last week…? Well, he wasn't alone.'

Alice's heart was pounding heavily as she arranged her features into an expression which she hoped gave no clue to the fact sick dread was tying her stomach in tight painful knots.

Sophie seemed to find the silence enough encouragement to continue, which was just as well, because if she'd changed her mind at this point Alice would have felt obliged to wring the information out of her!

'This woman—well, girl, really…Italian…was with him…' Sophie looked so unhappy that if Alice hadn't been so busy coping with a strong urge to throw up she might well have felt sorry for her.

'Beautiful, of course?'

Sophie nodded, visibly unsure of how to read her sister's wry response. She didn't look devastated. Perhaps Greg had been wrong and Alice wasn't in love with Gabe. She gave a sigh of relief.

'The MacAllisters know her family, apparently. Her father did a lot of business with Greg's dad in the early days. She'd been staying in their family's place in the mountains, but they had the builders in or something.'

No prizes for guessing she hadn't been staying there alone! Alice worried that *rigor mortis* had set in to her facial muscles, which were locked in a carefully neutral smile.

'Greg says that Rosanna and Gabe have always been friends, but nothing romantic...' she added hastily.

Until now.

'He didn't act as if... But she was running around after him, fussing as though he was incapable of lifting a teacup. *Lean on me, Gabe...*' she mimicked, adopting an attractive Italian purr. '*You shouldn't exert yourself, darling*—I expect she wanted him to preserve his energy for later!' she observed cuttingly. Then she broke off, her eyes widening in dismay. 'That is—I've no idea if they were actually...you know...'

'Lean on me...?' Alice questioned blankly. Gabriel wasn't the sort of man who went in much for leaning. Or maybe with the sexy Rosanna it was different...

'Exactly! I know he's hurt his ankle, but that doesn't make the man incapable!'

Obviously not! 'He's hurt his ankle?' Under the circumstances logic told her she ought to revel in the idea of

Gabriel's pain and discomfort instead of feeling a sharp wave of anxiety. She was clearly certifiable.

'Yeah, didn't I say?' Sophie said, her mind clearly on more important matters. 'He's getting around all right with a stick now, and he's driving again. There's probably nothing in it, but I thought you had the right to know. Actually,' she added as an afterthought, 'I quite liked her.'

Like I needed to know that!

'It's nothing to me who Gabriel carries on with.' Amazingly she even managed a very creditable carefree laugh—maybe a bit *too* carefree, if Sophie's suddenly suspicious expression was anything to go by. 'We didn't part on the best of terms.'

In fact she should have expected him to respond to rejection like this. Her thoughts bridled away from the shameful fact it had been more than a simple rejection that night at the hospital—she'd gone for his Achilles' heel and they'd both known it. She brushed aside the guilty pang.

He had women drooling all over him wherever he went. Why should Gabriel MacAllister waste his time fretting for someone like her?

'I appreciate you felt you had to tell me.' Her chin tilted to a defiantly proud angle. There was something awfully undignified about displaying a broken heart. 'I know Gabriel is your future brother-in-law, but there are much more interesting things to think about right now. For instance, what am I going to do with Will on Saturday?' she enquired briskly. 'Tea, Mum. Just what I need.'

Actually, if anyone had offered her a stiff whisky at the moment she'd probably have overlooked the fact she couldn't bear the stuff. She smiled at her mother, who was looking a bit red around the eyes.

'I was just saying Sophie has invited everyone we know,

so there isn't going to be a babysitter to be had for love nor money.'

Sophie smiled, but her eyes remained troubled.

'No problem. That's all been thought of. They've got loads of friends with babies and children, so there's going to be a crêche with proper nannies and a nursery. So all the mums can whoop it up till dawn.'

'Dawn might be a bit optimistic.' Alice stifled a yawn. She'd done an extra night's work that week, to help cover holiday leave, and now more than ever, since his illness, she hated leaving Will.

Sophie's detailed description of the sumptuous buffet which would be offered them passed over her head. All she could think of, all she'd been able to think of since she'd heard the news, was that the day after tomorrow she was going to see Gabriel again! And Sophie's revelations had only made matters more difficult.

She might have made a grand exit, oozing spite and poisonous animosity, but he'd obviously had help to recover from her wounding words. Alice still couldn't forgive herself. He'd given her a glimpse of his vulnerabilities when he'd told her of his feelings about his father and she'd used that insight to wound him. The vindictiveness troubled her; it just wasn't like her!

When she closed her eyes she could still see the frozen expression of startled hurt on Gabriel's face when she'd flung that below-the-belt jibe about his father, in that split second before all expression had been wiped clean. She'd spend the time they'd been apart wishing the words unsaid.

There was no way to wrap it up—she was jealous as hell! Perverse, or what? Anyone would think she—who had already suffered a rotten marriage—was hanging out for a husband. Any husband, let alone one who only wanted her because she was the mother of his child. But what she wanted might very well be irrelevant, she reminded herself heavily. His silence even before she'd known there was a Rosanna was eloquent proof that he hadn't forgotten or forgiven. He'd clearly had second thoughts.

She ought to be grateful to Sophie for making her see how truly hopeless the whole situation was. Gratitude was the last thing she felt as she sat nodding woodenly when her sister paused for breath.

'Alice?'

She experienced an odd sense of *déjà vu* and almost dropped the phone. 'Yes, it's me,' she croaked hoarsely.

Listening to his voice told her nothing, but it did demonstrate humiliatingly clearly how his voice above all others could send her entire nervous system into overload. She hadn't realised until this moment how much she had missed the sound of his voice.

'Are you well…and Will?'

His politeness made her want to weep. It occurred to her that the teasing wordplay between them which had infuriated her had also made her feel special.

'Yes, yes, we're fine.'

'About tonight. I was hoping you could come over to the hotel early. My parents would really like to meet you and Will.'

'You've told them?'

'Is that a problem?' His cold tone made it sound as though he cared less.

'Of course you have. It's just Sophie didn't say anything…' Her voice trailed away. If that had been strictly true she wouldn't feel so racked with jealousy.

She shook her head and tried to compose her thoughts, and not to think about a dark-haired woman running her fingers over… Stop it, Ally! Naturally he'd told his parents they had a grandchild. What was she thinking of…? Gabriel, almost to the exclusion of all else. The answer came back shockingly clear.

'I wasn't sure if you still wanted…'

'Nothing can alter the fact Will is my son, Alice.' He sounded tersely impatient at her denseness.

'It's been over a fortnight…' Her voice came out low, tremulous and horrifyingly *needy*.

She could hear the hiss of his startled intake of breath clearly down the line. He must have heard the needy part too, she realised, almost beside herself with mortification.

'Will has been asking for you.'

As diversions went this one was custom-made for the occasion. When he spoke she could hear the eagerness in his voice; it brought an emotional lump to her throat.

'Really?'

'Really, Gabriel.' He did love their baby. She couldn't punish him because he didn't love her.

'What does he call me?'

'The nice man,' she told him huskily.

'It's better than the horrid man.' She might have imagined the wistful quality in his deep voice.

'Definitely. That's how he refers to the entire medical profession—which demonstrates an appalling lack of gratitude considering they saved his life.' Her voice sounded high-pitched and ever so slightly manic to her own worried ears. She raced on to fill the awkward gap which was developing. 'All Will knows is they stuck the needles in him, poor little soul…'

'Children need continuity, Alice.'

'Will's quite adaptable really.'

'I thought me going away would help…I know it was what you wanted.'

If only he really knew what I want, she thought, closing

her eyes and pressing her forehead against one tightly balled fist. If only *I* knew!

'I was wrong. I know you can't stomach the idea of marrying me, but I'm still going to be involved with Will.'

'The things I said, Gabriel—'

'It doesn't matter now.' His cold voice cut across her faltering apology. 'I'll send a car for you around six. Does that suit?'

'No...yes...I mean, that's fine.' She heard the line go dead, but it was several minutes later before she unpeeled her sweaty fingers from the receiver.

She fastened the safety gate across the nursery door and raced down to answer the urgent ring of the doorbell.

'I thought,' she said, staring at him blankly, tall and unthinkably gorgeous in black tie, 'you were sending a car. I'm not ready.' She pulled the gaping lightweight robe tight around her unfettered bosom. 'I was,' she explained stiltedly, 'but Will spilt a beaker of blackcurrant juice over my dress.'

Her lower lip wobbled and she caught it savagely between her teeth. It wasn't like her to get upset about trivial things like a spoiled outfit, but tonight was no normal night.

He shrugged and stepped past her into the hallway, leaning lightly on his cane. 'It doesn't matter.'

'Of course it matters!' Only a man could think otherwise. 'I don't want to be late to meet your parents, and what do you think I have? A wardrobe full of designer clothes?' She doubted the exclusive label on the stunning outfit Sophie had proudly modelled would be the only designer label on display tonight. 'I've no idea what I'm going to wear now.'

'What about that nice thing you were wearing at the church fête, the blue one?' Gabriel elaborated helpfully.

Her eyes skimmed his face suspiciously. By God, he was actually serious!

'That was an old chainstore beach dress at least three years old,' she told him, torn between tears and laughter.

'So what's the problem? You looked beautiful in it,' he told her matter-of-factly.

Alice felt the telltale pink glow of gratification spread over her face. 'It isn't suitable,' she managed eventually, trying to disguise the fact his compliment sent bubbles of pleasure infinitely more potent than champagne zinging through her bloodstream. This is the man that went straight from your arms to a less critical and probably more skilful substitute, she reminded herself brutally. Show some pride!

'Where's Will?'

'Playing in his room and hopefully staying clean. Before you go to him, Gabriel, there's something I want to tell you—I tried on the phone…'

'I think you've already made your point very eloquently. You don't want to marry me—fine! However, despite my gene pool, I'm going to make one hell of father. And one hell of an enemy,' he warned quietly, 'if you try and derail me.'

What had he said to her…? Information was power? Pity he'd not kept that in mind when he'd spilled his life story to her. He'd never revealed that much of himself to anyone. It had never crossed his mind that Alice of all people would use that information maliciously. What she'd said had been bad, but it was *who* had said it that had really hurt.

'Don't worry, Alice, betrayal is a cold fact of life, I just lost track of that important fact for a while.'

'Will you just shut up and listen for a moment?' She gave the words the full benefit of her healthy lung capacity.

He blinked, and then nodded slowly.

'Get it off your chest before you explode.' If her emotional bosom-heaving got much more dramatic she was going to explode quite literally from that flimsy little wrap thing. The woman had made it quite clear she despised him as a father, she'd rejected him as a lover, and all he could think about was what she had on—if anything—underneath! He was fast becoming a candidate for the funny farm!

'I was a bitch to you. No two ways about it,' she told him frankly. The fact that he was a faithless swine didn't lessen the awfulness of what she'd said.

There was no comforting denial forthcoming, but she did have his attention, and it wasn't as if she'd expected him to rush to her defence. I owe him some sort of explanation, she reminded herself as her resolve began to waver.

'I've met bitches, even slept with a few before and survived.' The crucial difference was he'd never made the mistake of falling in love with them.

His light dismissive words of reassurance made Alice squirm, but then she concluded they had probably been meant to do just that. She gritted her teeth, determined now to reveal all.

'For a long time Oliver and I had been trying for a baby.'

Did she actually think this was something he wanted to think about? 'Is this relevant?' His hand tightened on the shiny polished newel post.

'Do you really think I'd be discussing it if it wasn't?' She glared at him incredulously. He looked distant and cold. *'This isn't easy!'* she told him forcibly from between clenched teeth. 'I'm trying to apologise.' She chewed nervously on her lower lip.

His firm lips twitched unexpectedly. Anything less apologetic than her stormy flushed face and jutting soft chin would be hard to imagine.

'In that case…'

'I'd imagined so often how it would be when I finally got…' The faint quiver of her lips was sternly quelled, and, frowning, she hunched her shoulders forward defensively. The words lurched out, gathering speed with each successive syllable. 'Well, when it did happen it wasn't like that at all. I didn't want to believe it at first…I *couldn't* be carrying a baby when I didn't know the father's name. It felt like a nightmare. Then when I couldn't pretend it wasn't happening I kept thinking…' She closed her eyes and swallowed. 'I kept thinking it would probably be for the best if something happened and I lost it…'

She opened her eyes, exhaled audibly and bit her lip, wondering absently why it felt so sore. Now he knew her terrible secret. She couldn't risk looking at him—especially now. She fixed her eyes on the magnolia-emulsioned wall behind him. What possessed me to use such a dull colour? she wondered.

Carefully she dabbed her tongue to the dots of moisture she could feel spring out along her upper lip. 'When something almost did happen it felt as if I'd wished it true.' The guilt even now was a solid lump of self-disgust in her belly. 'I also realised then how much I wanted that baby—Will. Hearing you say what you did, in all innocence, to Greg brought it all back—the guilt thing. I overreacted, to put it mildly, and you took the brunt of it. As for complaining that you only wanted to marry me for Will's sake—it wasn't as if you'd ever pretended otherwise.' This pragmatic confession cost her almost as much as sharing her deepest darkest secret had.

'I didn't, did I…?'

This wasn't quite the reaction she'd been expecting. To her surprise there had been none of the condemnation in his voice she'd been steeling herself for. There was *something* in his tone, though, that brought her eyes involuntarily back to his face. If he felt contempt he was hiding it well. Unfortunately for her raging curiosity he was hiding everything else too!

'You didn't have to tell me that.' It had never struck him until he'd listened to her halting disclosure just how desperately frightened she must have been, finding herself carrying a stranger's child—his child. What a terribly lonely secret it must have been.

'I've never told anyone else,' she confided gruffly. 'It's not the sort of thing you boast about. I'd better go and check on Will.' Gathering up the long skirt of her robe, she went past him and up the stairs two at a time.

Never told anyone else...*she told me!*

Alice was opening the safety gate stretched across the open nursery doorway when Gabriel came up behind her. Will, dressed for the occasion in cute blue dungarees and matching shirt, saw them both. He abandoned his tower of colourful bricks and raced across the room towards them on his sturdy legs.

He laughed out loud with delight as Gabriel swept him dizzily high in the air above his head.

'He's not afraid of anything,' Alice explained to Gabriel, torn between despair and pride at this trait in her son.

'Except jabs, hey, mate?'

'You're not using your stick!' she accused. She'd imagined the upper storey would be off-limits to him.

He slid her an amused look, as if suspecting her thoughts. 'I'm almost mended. The cane's just to get the sympathy vote.'

Alice snorted, just in case he assumed he'd had hers. 'I'll be as quick as possible.'

She shot a surreptitious glance up at Gabriel. His expression was nothing short of besotted as he looked at their son. She came to a spontaneous decision.

'You stay with...*Daddy*, Will.' She dropped a quick kiss on his soft baby cheek and fled without looking to see if Gabriel had registered the significance of what she'd said.

If she had been looking she would have seen something that some people would have considered an outright impossibility—a suspiciously misty sheen in his liquid dark eyes as he hugged his son fiercely to him.

Most of Alice's wardrobe was draped haphazardly across her bed when there was a gentle tap on the door. Gabriel came in, stooped slightly to one side as he held their son's tiny hand.

'He was asking for you.'

Alice wasn't entirely sure she believed him, Will was showing very little interest in his mother, but she didn't contest the statement. Will climbed clumsily onto the bed and she rescued a short—*the* short—black number she wore for virtually every social event she attended.

'It'll have to be this,' she said, holding it up.

'What about this one?' She watched, a sinking feeling deep in her stomach, as Gabriel extracted a soft misty blue backless number.

'Is something wrong?' There was a faint but discernible blue discoloration around her lips and her expression suggested he was holding a semi-automatic not a skimpy frock.

'I've only worn it once. The night...'

Gabriel caught on immediately—he didn't need a diagram to fill in the details.

Why the hell did I carry on pushing the marriage ticket when I half suspected that she'd had a marriage that had gone sour? he wondered with self-disgust. Great strategy, Gabe! What Sophie had let slip last night—not so accidentally, he suspected—about the husband having a long-standing drink problem made his insensitivity all the more dumb. If he was going to get anywhere he'd have to show a little more finesse. Obviously mentioning marriage was strictly off the agenda until he could show her that it didn't have to be that way. Like I'm the expert! he thought, his lips curling in a self-derisive but determined grimace.

Alice's chin went up. How crazy was it to be intimidated by a piece of cloth? A piece of cloth with associations, admittedly. She'd been so optimistic when she'd chosen it, spending what had seemed—and still did, for that matter—a reckless amount on the beautiful piece of silk, that it was going to be a new start. It had seemed significant that Oliver had wanted to celebrate their anniversary more elaborately than usual.

'I'll wear it.'

'Good girl.'

'I could do with some space.' She raised one eyebrow and looked at him expectantly. Was he going to make her spell it out? 'We're already late.'

'I could help.'

'Yes, by keeping Will amused.'

'I was thinking more along the lines of zips. I really am very good with them.'

No doubt he'd had a lot of practice over the last few weeks. She felt queasy at the thought. 'I hope you're not reading anything stupid into my brief flirtation with humility,' she ground out as he grinned back calmly at her.

'I hate apologising too,' he commiserated. 'But you did it with style. I think we should put all that behind us.'

He *sounded* generous. 'Fine…' I think!

'And you don't have to worry about me pestering you to marry me.'

'That's nice to know.' Her smile was grim. I don't need two guesses as to what or rather *who* has brought about this turnaround!

'But that doesn't mean anything else has to change.'

'Are you suggesting we still...?' Her voice rose to an indignant squeak.

'Remain lovers. Of course.' He was prepared to go slowly, but not *that* slowly. Fortunately his family had put his extreme bad humour down to his frustration over his limited mobility. If they'd known the true reason he'd been going slowly out of his mind he doubted they'd have been quite so understanding.

'I only stayed with Oliver out of ignorance when he was having an affair, not because I have deeply liberal ideas or a warm understanding personality!'

'Am I being slow?'

'No, just optimistic,' she snarled. 'Sophie told me about your...your...Rosanna!'

He looked cautious rather than outright concerned when she made her triumphant announcement. Actually, Alice had rarely felt less triumphant in her life!

'What exactly did she tell you?' he fished delicately. For a minute there he'd thought that Rosanna had ignored his request to keep quiet.

'She didn't go into the sordid details.'

'What a relief,' he responded drily. There was curiosity in his face as he watched her. She didn't look happy.

'I'm not about to be your girl in this particular port!' she hissed angrily.

Gabriel, who recognised jealousy when it was thrust under his nose, felt happier than he had done in weeks. 'Are you saying you demand exclusivity?' he enquired worriedly. He counted silently to five before she predictably reached detonation point.

'Bloody right I do!' she exploded.

'Fine.'

Frowning, Alice watched him tickle their son into a state

of delirium. I just hope he throws up over Gabriel and not himself, she thought viciously.

'What do you mean...*fine*?'

'You want exclusivity—you have it.'

'Just like that?'

'You're seeing problems where there aren't any. I draw the line at signing my name in blood, but my word's good in most places,' he boasted calmly.

His attitude perplexed her. 'What about Rosanna?'

'She'll want what's best for me,' he assured her confidently. 'And you,' he told her firmly as he began to walk towards the door, the giggling toddler over his shoulder, 'are the best thing for me, Alice.'

Alice was thrown into such disarray by this cryptic parting shot that she struggled for ten minutes before she finally managed the zip he'd been so eager to assist with.

CHAPTER EIGHT

'WAS that thunder?' Alice peered through the window up at a suspiciously leaden sky. The air-conditioning in the car offered a respite from the increasing humidity of the early evening.

The flickering glance from Gabriel's inky dark eyes made her abruptly aware she was nibbling daintily with betraying nervousness at one fingernail. She snatched her hand away; she hadn't bitten her nails since she was a teenager.

She was having a hard enough time matching up to the sexy image of the dress without regressing that far back! Though when she considered how tough it had been to quell the impulse to tug up the low neckline of the blue silk under Gabriel's silent scrutiny she wondered if she'd actually progressed much from those acne-ridden angst days!

She cast a quick furtive look at his profile from under the sweep of her lashes. As she rubbed her damp palms against her silk-covered thighs her breath came shallow and irregular. Even now just thinking about the way he had looked at her almost suffocated her with desire.

If she allowed herself to respond to the raw hunger in his eyes would he dismiss her just as casually as he had Rosanna once he'd lost interest? She didn't think she could bear it if their relationship degenerated towards platonic. She still hadn't recovered from his calm assertion he wouldn't sleep with any other women. True...it wasn't exactly an avowal of love...but... Her tortured brain felt numb as she tried to sort out his motivation—other than the obvious. It was the obvious fact that he wanted to make love to her that reduced her deductive powers to zero.

'Almost certainly. Don't worry, a car's the safest place to be in a storm. The lightning's safely earthed.'

'Aren't you the optimist?' she mocked. 'I wasn't actually planing on getting struck by lightning.'

'I think the point is it's not the sort of thing you can plan,' he told her drily.

'This is England,' she reminded him. 'We don't go in for extremes of weather...'

'You were saying?' he prompted maliciously, as hailstones the size of small pebbles began to hit the car.

'Wow! They're the size of golf balls.' She had to raise her voice against the cacophony. 'I've never seen anything like it. They won't smash the windscreen or anything, will they?'

'Unlikely.'

It was a well-known fact that the best way to teach a child fear was by example. So now, she decided, probably wasn't the time to confess she had never liked thunder. *Never* would be the time to confess any weaknesses to Gabriel! As for lightning! She tried not to cringe back in her seat when a flash illuminated the interior of the car.

Alice glared at his profile resentfully, perversely annoyed that she was hiding her fear so well that he didn't seem to appreciate she was scared out of her wits. She did gain a few grains of comfort from the fact that even if he wasn't clapping his hands in delight, like their son in the back seat, Gabriel didn't look overly concerned by the situation.

'I know a shortcut. Or perhaps we should stop and wait until it's over?'

'Just give me directions, Alice.'

Alice was pleased with the reply. She didn't want to be out here in the open any longer than strictly necessary.

Despite the fact that the rain, which had replaced the hail in bucketfuls, was making conditions appalling, Gabriel didn't seem to have any problem following her instructions. Progress down the narrow country lanes was slow—he got out to remove several fallen branches that had partially blocked the way—but steady.

'What,' Gabriel asked, eventually bringing the car to a halt on the crest of a sharp rise, 'is that?'

'A ford.' The small rivulet which normally trickled across the steep dip in the road did look a little more solid than normal, but he was making a fuss about nothing... Another few minutes and they'd be at the hotel, and one ordeal at least would be over. She could only cope with one at a time, thank you, and had no intention of even thinking about the next trial lined up for this evening until they were safely out of this storm.

'I can see that.' For some reason Gabriel suddenly appeared to find the sight of the water amusing. He was grinning in what she considered a maniacal sort of way. 'Not again! Is someone trying to tell me something?' he asked nobody in particular.

'If you knew it was a ford why did you ask?' she snapped. Between being spoken to like an idiot and the thunder, which sounded alarmingly close, she was not in the mood to be understanding. 'I don't think now is a good time to fall to pieces,' she added disapprovingly.

'Fall to pieces?' he echoed in bewilderment. He caught her meaning and started to laugh again.

'Share the joke—I could do with a good laugh.' Anyone who could find hilarity in this situation was seriously unbalanced!

'I'll try not to crack up completely,' he promised solemnly. 'Tell me, didn't it occur to you that it's not a good idea to ford a river in the middle of a cloudburst?'

'It isn't a river,' she told him scornfully. 'It's a stream.'

'I suggest, sweetheart, you take another look.'

Alice did, and swallowed. 'Well, it's a lot quicker than the long way around. Where are you going?' she added sharply as he opened the door a crack.

Gabriel pulled the door closed as he spoke, to cut out the industrial-strength howl of the elements outside. 'I'm going to see how deep it is.'

'You'll get wet.'

'And ruin my hair too, most probably…' he mocked, lifting his hand to the slick darkness of his damp hair. His numerous halts to clear the path had already wet him to the skin—she could see his skin plus the suggestion of dark body hair through the transparent whiteness of his wet shirt. Her skin, which always felt raw and unprotected when he was around, tingled uncomfortably as she averted her eyes.

'I tell you this ford is *always* passable,' she told him stubbornly.

'As much as I appreciate local knowledge, I'd prefer to confirm that for myself.'

The patronising smile made her hope he got very, very wet! So much for her opinion! *Typical!* she fumed silently as he slammed the door. It was then, staring at his broad superior back, that it came to her.

He'd look pretty stupid when she and Will were sitting comfortably on the other side of the stream. Smiling grimly—it was childish but satisfying to think of him being forced to wade across the water—she unclipped her seat belt and slid over into the driver's seat.

She had a flashing image of his stark white-faced anger and heard a snatched yell and warning as the car gathered speed on the steep incline and slid smoothly past him. Her confidence remained high as the car entered the narrow band of water. It was a manoeuvre she'd done countless times in her life, though never in anything nearly so luxurious as this car.

The problem was the water, normally a trickle, really never had been this deep, or the current so strong on those countless occasions. The Mercedes made it to the centre of the stream before it stopped completely.

I've done it now!

Alice had Will, who, sensing his mother's distress, had begun to loudly wail, on her knee by the time Gabriel reached the side of the car. He banged on the window to get her attention.

'I can't open that door!' she yelled loudly against the din.

'No, there's a branch or something jammed up against this side,' he shouted back. 'No! Don't get out the other side,' he warned sharply as she moved towards the passenger door. 'The current's too strong—you might stumble carrying Will before I get around.'

Alice swallowed as visions of herself and Will washed away by a raging current flashed through her mind. She knew this to be a humiliating, grovelling situation rather than the serious life-threatening variety, but all the same she couldn't stop the flicker of fear that raced through her body. It was at times like this, she reflected grimly, that you remembered it paid to be humble when you pitted yourself against the elements even in temperate-climated England!

Gabriel wiped the window clear of water. 'Open the window!' he mouthed clearly.

Alice didn't need a second bidding because the car—several tens of thousands' worth of solid metal—lurched sideways as he spoke. 'Oh, baby,' she muttered under her breath. 'What have I done to you?' She kissed Will's dark head apologetically.

It only took a second for her face to be drenched by the rain that came through the open window. The moisture was cold on her bare shoulders; she'd used the silk wrap that matched her dress to protectively swaddle Will. She kept his face cradled by her hand, turned protectively towards her breast.

'It won't go all the way down.'

'I'll write a letter to the manufacturers.'

'So you were right. I expect that makes you very happy!' Sometimes, she reflected, I just can't believe the stuff that comes out of my mouth.

Gabriel, standing almost thigh-deep in a muddy torrent, blinked, her sheer bloody-minded unreasonableness robbing him of breath for a second. 'Oh, sure,' he drawled, blowing a drip of water of the tip of his nose. 'I'm delirious! Now, pass Will to me through the window.'

'I'm sorry about your car,' she muttered, as the transfer was successfully achieved. Miraculously, a few words into his son's ear and Will seemed to have recovered his usual high spirits.

His scathing look suggested she'd reached new heights of inanity. 'Now you.'

'Now me what…?'

'Squeeze through the window and I'll grab you.'

'I don't want to squeeze through the window and I definitely don't want you grabbing me,' she informed him with a distinct lack of gratitude.

With the demeanour of someone seeking divine intervention, Gabriel rolled his eyes skywards. 'I'm a very patient man,' he ground out slowly, 'but you are pushing me. Get out through the damned window, Alice! *Now!*' he bellowed.

She sniffed. 'There's absolutely no need,' she informed him with dignity, 'to be abusive.'

She abandoned all claims to dignity during the next awkward manoeuvre.

'I'm stuck!' she told him at the point where her hips seemed jammed fast in the narrow opening. He was using his free hand to support her waist and she was suspended head-down with an excellent view of the freshly scratched paintwork.

'Come on, thunder thighs,' he urged reassuringly, 'you can do it.'

Thunder thighs! It was probably that wrathful breath she sucked in that enabled her to finally wriggle clear.

'Watch out!' he warned sharply as with a cry of triumph she tried to put her feet down. She hadn't made allowances for her unstable centre of gravity and her laugh was cut short as she did a neat forward roll in mid-air and landed flat on her back in the swollen stream.

Spluttering and spitting out weeds, she struggled to her feet. She smoothed the strands of drenched hair from her face and removed a large leafy twig from the bodice of her dress. Wiping the dripping moisture from her face, she unwittingly smeared fresh mud down her cheeks.

'Well!' she managed breathlessly. 'Are we going to stay here all night?' If he laughed, and from the faint quiver around his mouth that was a definite possibility, she'd kill him!

So saying, she picked up her sodden skirts and strode purposefully towards the bank, only feet away. Actually she was quite glad when Gabriel caught her up and insisted she keep hold of him to steady herself; the water, though not excessively deep, was flowing strongly.

'Remind me of this next time you mention the words

shortcut,' he said, when they had all reached the muddy bank. 'Here, hold Will.' He thrust the baby into her arms.

'Don't go back in there!' she yelled as he strode towards the bank once more.

'Your concern for my welfare is touching.' The quirk of one dark brow was silently sardonic. 'Don't worry, I'll be back in time to throttle you with my own bare hands,' he promised darkly.

Naturally he'd ignored her. Alice spent the tense minutes he was away mentally tearing his character to shreds and trying to distract a squirming Will, who seemed to think it would be a grand idea to follow his father.

When Gabriel returned, carrying the articles he'd extracted from the car boot above his head, she noticed he was limping. A bit late in the day she recalled his ankle injury. Despite the fact the last way in the world she felt towards Gabriel was maternal, she was swamped by an unexpected flood of warm, mushy protective feelings.

'Here, wrap Will in this.' He handed her a man-sized waterproof.

'Thank you,' she said stiffly. 'Your leg…'

'Don't fuss, woman,' he advised her sharply.

Fine. He didn't want sympathy, he wouldn't get any. He could get…get…gangrene for all she cared! She couldn't help shooting a worried look towards his ankle.

'Here, you take this.' The jacket he slid over her shoulders wasn't waterproof, but it was warm. 'I just need this.' He pulled a mobile phone from the pocket. 'First we'd better get well away from these trees. With my recent track record I'll probably draw the first stray lightning bolt.'

She looked at him cautiously. He hadn't started ranting and raving about her stupidity yet, but it was only a matter of time, she gloomily predicted. Worse was the knowledge she deserved it. What had made her behave so irrationally?

They moved up to the top of the slope away from the wooded hollow, Gabriel speaking into his phone as they went. He slid it back into his pocket and turned to face her.

'That's sorted. They're sending out a car for us and contacting a garage to tow the car out.' He held out his hands. 'Let me take him; he must be heavy.'

Her shoulders were aching—Will was a big solid child. 'I suppose you're pretty mad?' She looked at the semi-submerged car and winced. The men she knew were pretty protective about their cars, and none of them had anything half as classy or expensive as that one!

'Is that a question or an accusation?'

Alice pushed a strand of wet hair from her eyes. She was pretty conscious of the fact Gabriel was due some comprehensive grovelling.

'Actually, I'm past mad.' *Mad* didn't cover the visceral lurch of terror he'd felt when he'd seen her drive past him into the river. He'd like to think this reaction had been largely due to his recent brush with death of the watery variety in Italy, but he knew otherwise. Even the remote possibility of losing his newly discovered family had aroused more fear in him than anything else in his life.

'It's never normally that deep.'

'So you mentioned.' The urgent desire to strangle the life out her with his own hands had passed. Other desires hadn't! The weight of the water had pulled the bodice of her dress a couple of inches lower, revealing the merest suggestion of one rosy nipple. On reflection he decided not to burden her with this knowledge.

She gave a sigh of defeat. 'All right, I'm sorry…I'm very sorry I drove your car into the stream.'

'River,' he prompted her lightly.

He wanted his pound of flesh—he could have it! 'River,' she agreed with difficulty. 'I'll pay for any damage.'

'The suit…the shoes…' he reminded her, looking at the remains of his sartorial fashion statement.

'Them too.'

He whistled lightly through his teeth, much to Will's delight. 'That could come to a hefty total.' He whistled once more, this time the ear-piercing variety for his son's benefit.

Alice watched as Will gazed at his father with predictable slave-like adoration through the peephole in his forest-green waterproof cocoon. Like mother like son, she thought dismally.

'And you being so financially strapped need restitution right away.' This was the sort of irresistible situation made to measure for an opportunist like Gabriel. Any second now he was going to make some smart-arse payment-in-kind sort of comment.

'Next week will be fine.' He watched her scornfully superior expression fade dramatically. Chagrin formed her lips into a quivering pout before the deliciously rounded chin came up.

'Fine.' Anyone would think she'd been looking forward to his blackmail!

'Everything's fine, then.'

She folded her arms across her chest.

'Don't look so sour—you were right. I was going to…'

'Going to what?' she enquired frigidly.

'Ask for payment in kind. But it's kind of difficult to work out how many…payments, if you get my drift?'

She did. 'Don't be delicate on my account.'

'How many would be worth a top-of-the-range car? That's right, stamp your feet,' he approved warmly. 'Nothing better to get the circulation moving. In fact I'll join you.' He did, much to Will's delight.

Alice watched him perform his impromptu war dance.

He moved with careless feral grace to the imaginary tune in his head. Head thrown back to let the rain stream over his brown laughing face, fronds of gleaming jet-black hair were plastered close to his skull.

'You're disgusting, crude and vulgar!' Beautiful, wild and awesome. Her heart was pounding in her breast; she was breathless with admiration. He really was the most beautiful man.

Gabriel stopped, even though a laughing Will was vocal in his encouragement. A wide white grin split his handsome face. The absurdity of the bizarre situation suddenly hit her…her lips twitched. Suddenly they were all laughing.

Alice's sides ached. Her legs felt weak, and as she staggered they collided, the small boy sandwiched between them. She looked up into Gabriel's face and watched the humour fade away.

The last bubble of laughter died in her throat. 'I don't know what made me do it,' she confessed huskily. 'I'm not normally so… You make me…'

'A little crazy?' he suggested, his mouth quirking in a fascinating lop-sided smile, though his eyes still remained grave. 'Join the club.'

A particularly loud crash of thunder ruined the expectant intimacy of the moment and made Alice leap several inches into the air.

'Are you by any chance frightened of thunder?' he asked, when she eventually lifted her head off his chest.

'My, you're so quick,' she murmured admiringly. Gabriel had a satisfyingly solid sort of chest for these occasions. Not that she made a habit of scuttling for the nearest manly bosom during moments of crisis. 'I prefer to view my storms from the safety of a dark cupboard,' she told him frankly.

'You don't find there's something...I don't know... stimulating about the raw elements?'

'No, I don't!' she told him positively.

'Not even a little bit stimulating...?' he suggested silkily.

They were standing close enough for Alice's quivering little sigh to be clearly audible.

He hefted Will, whose sleepy head had drooped against his shoulder, a little more firmly in one arm before taking Alice's round chin in his free hand. His strong fingers sent delicious shivers all the way down to her toes.

'I think we should move in together.' There was an uncharacteristic urgency in his deep voice, but Alice didn't notice. His abrupt words had sent her brain into instant shutdown.

'I thought you'd dropped the marriage idea,' she managed hoarsely. Conflict was written clearly on her upturned rain-washed features.

His shoulders lifted in an impatient shrug. 'We don't need a marriage certificate to move in together. People do it all the time.'

How could he joke abut something so momentous? she wondered. Perhaps it wasn't momentous to him—just convenient. I don't want to be convenient, an inner voice wailed. I want to be loved, cherished, adored!

A noise made Gabriel glance up, and he swore. It was not the moment for the cavalry to arrive, but it had done anyway, in the form of his brother driving a lumbering four-wheel drive. Greg leapt from the vehicle, leaving the engine running, and loped energetically over to the stranded trio.

'Is everyone all right? My God, you both look terrible!' He was wearing a drover's-coat-style waxed raincoat which reached his ankles.

'You remember Greg, of course, he's the tactful one.'

Gabriel reached down and pulled the flapping sides of the jacket he had draped over her shoulders together.

Impatiently Alice automatically looked down to see what he was doing. And she not only saw what he was doing, she saw why! He responded with a virtuous smile to her pink-cheeked indignant glare.

He bent forward and spoke softly in her ear. 'I don't like sharing everything with my little brother.'

Alice felt her face flush—she felt an all-over flush! 'At least Greg didn't tell me I had big hips.' *Thunder thighs* wasn't the sort of slur a girl could let pass.

'That was a joke of course.' Should I have said compliment? he wondered uneasily. Women were a bit touchy when it came to thighs.

'Do you see me laughing?' She was glad to see that for once she was able to keep him wondering.

'It might be an idea if you continue this discussion inside.'

'Greg's worried about his hair.'

'Take no notice of him. You've got lovely hair, Greg, I expect he's jealous,' Alice suggested sympathetically, looking at Greg's pale gold carefully arranged tresses, which she felt no desire whatever to run her fingers through.

'Enjoy it while you've got it, Greg. Genetics…'

Greg glared at his brother, who, at thirty-four, was the smug possessor of a dense head of hair, whilst they both knew Robert MacAllister was follically challenged, and Greg had definitely inherited his dad's hairline.

'How did you come to drive your car into the river?'

Gabriel glanced at Alice as he helped her up into the high vehicle and passed the sleepy toddler to her. 'A momentary lapse of judgement,' he said, holding her gaze.

'I didn't think you had those,' Greg responded with a grin as his brother climbed in beside him.

'He didn't. I did. I drove the car into the stre...river.'

'Early Christian martyr material!' Gabriel exclaimed, slapping his forehead. 'I was trying to do the gentlemanly thing.'

'I'm quite capable of accepting responsibility for my own actions, thank you.'

'Me too.' Gabriel responded instantly to her crisp retort by turning in his seat and letting his eyes deliberately rest on Will's cherubic face. 'If people will let me.'

Greg appeared cheerfully oblivious to the undertones. 'I've got instructions to get you back quick-smart. Rosanna flipped when we said you'd ended up in river. I reckon the woman's not all there.' He tapped his forehead significantly. 'She's gone all dramatic and Latin. Every time anyone says anything to her she starts crying.'

Gabriel caught his head in his hands and groaned. 'I should have thought. Poor Rosanna. Put your foot down, Greg.'

Thought what? His Latin lover...correction...*beautiful* Latin lover would be beside herself if she suspected any harm had come to him? Alice felt sick with humiliation. She could have forgiven a lot, but he hadn't even bothered to hide his anxiety to get back to her. The lying two-faced snake in the grass!

'I'm so sorry I'm keeping you from your guests, Gabriel.'

Her eyes rested scornfully on the back of his neck. It was a pity that Sophie had stopped short of informing her that the lovely Rosanna had followed Gabriel back to England when she'd spilt the rest of the dirt.

Hearing the ice in her voice, he spun around in his seat. 'I came to pick you up myself because I wanted to be with you and Will.'

'Of course you did!' she agreed with a hollow laugh. 'Wc'rc a package deal.'

And if we weren't I'd be nothing more than another notch in his bedpost. Would she never learn? Two minutes in his company and she was eagerly believing everything his silver tongue threw at her

'Meaning…?' he snarled. What did he have to do? Present her with his beating heart on a bloody silver platter!

Greg cleared his throat uncomfortably and Gabriel rounded on him with a harsh, 'Have you got something to say?'

'No…no, not me. I'm not even here.' Looking as if he'd prefer to be anywhere else, he slunk farther down in his seat.

'Despite rumours to the contrary—' at this point he looked daggers at his brother '—I'm not sleeping with Rosanna.'

She was aiming for utmost irritation value with her tinkling laughter—and if the febrile pulse-beat in his lean jaw was anything to go by, she'd succeeded!

'That no doubt accounts for the dark shadows under your eyes.'

Gabriel's jaw clenched and his eyes swept icily over her angry face. 'You're jealous,' he announced flatly.

Alice went white. 'In your dreams!' she breathed wrathfully. 'I don't care if you keep a harem you…you serial Casanova!'

Gabriel winced slightly and touched one ear gingerly. 'If decibels were uninterest I'd believe you,' he agreed drily. 'You'll wake Will if you get much more uninterested. And, just for the record, the only reason I've lost any sleep just lately is you and your bloody-minded intransigence.'

Greg gave a heartfelt sigh of relief. 'We're here,' he announced half apologetically as he pulled up on the forecourt of the country house hotel.

He hadn't really expected anyone to take any notice of him, so it didn't come as too much of a shock when they acted as if he was invisible.

'Intransigence translates roughly as anyone who has the temerity not to fall in with your plans.'

'I've fallen over backwards to do things your way!'

'The sad part is he believes it!'

Greg, who didn't want any part in the conversation, determinedly avoided her eyes. He jumped out of the vehicle at the same moment their reception committee arrived.

'Oh, you poor dears!'

Gabriel had his mother's eyes—only hers weren't hard, unyielding and dangerous. All Alice's fears about this meeting faded away; suddenly it didn't matter that she had probably never looked more bedraggled in her life. The woman standing beside the open door of the Land Rover had kind smiling eyes, and she exuded a warmth that Alice felt immediately. Clare MacAllister held out her arms to receive the sleeping child and Alice automatically relinquished her burden.

She scarcely had time to register the other people as she stepped out onto the gravelled forecourt before a tall voluptuous raven-haired figure wearing a diaphanous wrap flung herself weeping at Gabriel. He visibly reeled under the flood of Italian.

He responded in the same language and then eventually said, in a voice which bore definite signs of irritation, 'I'm fine…everything's fine.'

Gabriel, with a weeping woman still attached to his chest, held both his hands palm flat up. He looked from the dark bent head to his mother's face.

Clare MacAllister's handsome face didn't reveal any sympathy for her eldest child's obvious plea for assistance. 'Well, what do you expect, Gabriel?' she asked tartly.

My thoughts exactly, Alice thought viciously. Unfortunately his embarrassment could in no way compare with the pain of her bruised and aching heart. Vaguely she was aware of Sophie coming up beside her and placing a warm blanket around her shoulders.

Her sister's soft sympathetic voice suggested they go inside, but Alice felt as if she was glued to the spot. She was unable to take her eyes off Gabriel with the weeping girl in his arms. Remember how this feels the next time you fall for the faithless rat's sweet lies, she told herself bleakly.

'Mother?'

'Don't play dumb with me, young man,' his mother advised sternly. 'Rosanna has told us all about what happened.'

The impossible happened. Gabriel blushed. To Alice, who had still secretly been nurturing unrealistic hopes that this awful situation might be explained away, this offered proof positive. So even he knew that seducing the young—*very* young—daughter of family friends was not something to be proud of. Alice was past caring if he had a conscience. It was one thing to suspect; it was quite another to have those worst fears confirmed so dramatically. How could a man who could seem so warm and caring be such a rat?

'No wonder the poor girl is distraught!'

The gruesome details could only make her feel more wretched, but somehow Alice couldn't turn her back on this sordid scene.

'I think perhaps Rosanna—' the young girl lifted her tear-drenched eyes at the sound of her name and gazed with spaniel-like devotion into his face '—is exaggerating what occurred,' he suggested blandly.

Alice shuddered. Just when she'd thought she couldn't feel more disgusted and let down! He was trying to weasel out of it! No trace of penitence, she decided, detecting only embarrassed irritation on his dark features. How could anyone looking at the beautiful distressed face of the Italian girl be so…so…callous? He was a monster! Alice quivered with outrage, and a strangled squeak of disgust which nobody seemed to notice escaped her stiff cold lips.

'I think not, Gabe, my dear, she's even got the video proof.'

Oh, God! At this point Alice's mouth fell open. In disbelief she tried to find her own horrified disgust mirrored on the faces around them. But amused tolerance seemed to be the most obvious and bewildering response. Was she a prude or were they all mad? Even my own sister! she thought numbly, looking at the silly affectionate grin on Sophie's face. Only Greg, standing just behind her, seemed to be equally bewildered.

Gabriel looked sharply down at the girl, who guiltily nodded her head. He lifted his shoulders, his lips curving in a quick rueful grin from which shame was noticeably absent.

'I thought we might hold a viewing later on, lad.' The tall burly figure of Robert MacAllister, his grin broad, stepped forward to slap Gabriel heartily on the back.

This was just too much for Alice, who had thought she was as tolerant and open-minded as the next person. She turned and fled into the plush interior of the country house hotel.

'Over my dead body!' she heard Gabriel respond as the heavy swing door closed behind her.

CHAPTER NINE

SOPHIE guided her stony-faced shivering sister towards her suite.

'I think you're taking this very well, Ally.'

Alice twirled, her drenched clothing sending out a flurry of wet drops that made Sophie take a cautious step backwards. She gave a hollow laugh.

'Do you?' If only she knew!

'Yes,' Sophie responded, a puzzled frown beginning to draw a line between her carefully darkened brows. 'I'd have been *devastated* if that had happened to my dress.'

'Dress?' Alice couldn't keep the incredulity out of her voice. She let Gabriel's sodden jacket slide off her shoulders. 'I don't give a damn about the dress.'

'Quite right too,' Sophie responded, unable to resist a quick complacent look down at the stunning gold sequinned creation she wore. 'I'm sure we can rustle you up something to wear—and as for your hair, it's nothing a quick shower won't fix.' She tried not to stare too obviously at the muddy smears adorning her sister's cheeks.

'I'm not staying for the party,' Alice choked.

Sophie's pretty face fell. 'You're not serious!' she wailed. 'This is my engagement party. You've *got* to be here, Ally! A cup of tea,' she suggested, desperately seeking inspiration. 'You'll feel much better after a nice cup of tea.'

If only a cup of tea *would* put right what was ailing her, Alice thought wistfully. 'I'm not in the party mood,' she responded, hardening her heart against the disappointment in his sister's face.

'But…but you have to!' There was a tap on the door. 'Gabe!' Sophie said with relief as the door opened. 'Will you tell Alice she must stay.'

'Alice, you must stay.'

He had to be the only person in the world who could squelch elegantly! 'You're dripping all over the carpet.' Alice vibrated cold hostility as he entered the room.

'Not as much as you are,' Gabriel responded, thinking antagonism not moisture. He looked pointedly at the widening damp patch developing on the deep luxurious carpet under her feet.

Alice looked away from his face when she felt the weak tears begin to form in her eyes. She sniffed loudly. 'I want Will!' she stated abruptly, with a tremor in her voice.

'Will's being taken care of,' Gabriel informed her calmly. 'He's flat out.'

'Do you think I'd take *your* word for anything?' When they lifted from her studied contemplation of the carpet her sapphire-blue eyes sparkled contemptuously.

A cautious hardness replaced the warmth in Gabriel's eyes.

'I'll go and check on him if you like,' Sophie suggested brightly. It was cowardly, she knew, but she wasn't quite sure how to cope with Ally when she was acting so weirdly. The oppressive pre-storm atmosphere they'd all had to endure that afternoon had been a whole lot more comfortable than the escalating tensions in this room.

Gabriel didn't wait until Sophie was out of the room. 'You're not still sulking over that stupid spat in the Land Rover, are you?' He'd waited thirty-plus years to tell a woman he loved her, and wasn't it just his bloody luck that she was looking at him as if he was a cockroach?

His weary drawl was the last straw. Alice saw red. 'You can ask that!' she boggled incredulously. 'After what I heard outside!'

'Oh, that.' He shuffled his feet uncomfortably. 'It's embarrassing, certainly,' he conceded gruffly. 'But it's no big deal. Anyone would have done the same.'

Only if anyone had the morals of a sleazy rat! Embarrassing!' she echoed incredulously. *'Embarrassing!'* Her voice went up a quivering outraged octave. Gabriel's puzzled frown deepened as he watched her inadequately covered bosom—great bosom—rise and fall dramatically. 'You think it's embarrassing to break a... God, Gabriel, she can't be any older than Sophie!' she choked in disgust.

'Have I got this right? You think I broke Rosanna's heart?' He couldn't prevent a hint of his amusement creeping into his voice. 'And all this righteous fury is purely altruistic, on behalf of her defiled innocence?' he suggested drily. 'Naturally the big green monster doesn't enter into it...?'

The pink spots on her pale cheeks deepened a guilty shade. How like Gabriel to somehow turn around the situation so that she felt she had to justify herself!

The teasing light died from his eyes, and as he held out his hands towards her Alice felt the sense of conflict raging within her deepen. She wanted so badly to take them.

Accepting her rejection with a shrug that was more casual than the frustrated glitter in his eyes, he let his hands fall away. 'Honestly, Alice, the only thing the kid feels for me is hero-worship...you know, gratitude. And damned inconvenient it is too,' he added with feeling.

This last little aside took her breath away. The man took arrogance right off the scale! 'Gratitude! Is that what women you deign to sleep with are meant to feel?'

If she hadn't known better she'd have fallen for the look

of bemused incomprehension that crossed his face. As she glared with dogged dislike up at him illumination swept across his drop-dead gorgeous features.

'Your faith in my integrity is touching, angel,' he ground out. 'I can understand Greg,' he added, half to himself, 'because he's my brother and an idiot...'

Alice found herself falling to the defensive once more. Her inner certainty was beginning to crumble. She shook her head angrily to dispel the doubts. She knew what she'd heard and seen—didn't she...?

'What about the video evidence?' she jeered, choking back a sob.

For ten seconds he stood there transfixed as he finally caught on to what she was implying. 'Video eviden...! You thought it was a video of me...me and...!' The laughter started as a rumble and got steadily stronger until his shoulders were heaving and tears of mirth were running down his face.

Either he was an Oscar-class actor or she'd got the wrong end of the stick with a vengeance! Her moral high ground suddenly felt rather shaky.

'If it wasn't a...'

'An X-rated video of me... My, oh, my, Alice...I'm shocked!'

He didn't look shocked; he looked amused and suddenly disturbingly complacent. 'All right, all right,' she cut in as he looked about ready to crack up again. She'd die of sheer humiliation if he started laughing at her again.

'I don't see what other sort of video they could have been talking about. And if it's all so innocent why didn't you want anyone to know about it?'

If she had been wrong, then what would Gabriel make of her wild rantings when he paused long enough to think about it? It didn't require a great leap of imagination to guess—terminal jealousy! She shifted her weight uneasily from one cold foot to the other as she contemplated this probability.

'I really don't want to talk about it,' he told her evasively.

'How convenient,' she sneered nastily.

'You're cold,' he observed, as her whole body was convulsed by a fresh shudder. 'Why don't you get out of those wet things before I try and defend my character?'

'Here?' She looked a little wildly around the plushly furnished bedroom.

'Sure, here. There aren't any hidden cameras.'

Alice flushed at this unkind jibe.

'And, before you ask, I've no intention of turning my back.'

'Fine!' She picked up the towels and robe Sophie had laid out on the bed and stalked to the *en suite* bathroom, locking the door with a defiant click behind her.

She had to clamp her hand over her mouth to stifle her shriek of horror when she looked in the mirror. Any man, even one driven wild with lust—which Gabriel wasn't—would have been able to resist her at that moment! The wild woman look! Take her worst scenario and times it by ten and you just about encompassed the full horror of her pale mud-streaked face and spiky tangled wet hair.

As tempting as the thought of a warm shower was, she was more concerned about discovering exactly what Gabriel was so reluctant to divulge. She washed her face, rubbed a towel roughly over her damp chilly skin until it was tingling and pink. She pulled on the big fluffy oversized hotel robe. With a sharp tug at the belt around her narrow waist, she left the sanctuary of the bathroom.

'That was quick.'

Alice blinked; so had he been. His clothes lay in an untidy wet heap and he had a far from adequate towel wound around his middle. Hell, but he had a good—no, a *great* body!

'What do you think you're doing?' she squeaked.

'Avoiding pneumonia…?'

Alice grunted. 'Perhaps you should avoid it in the privacy of your own room, not my sister's.'

'Oh, I think Sophie is much too wise to come back before she's sure you've cooled down.' There was a light tap on the door. 'Unfortunately the same can't be said for my mother,' he added in a wry aside as his parent entered the room.

'I hope I'm not interrupting anything.' She looked cheerfully from her son to Alice and back again.

'You are.'

'Not at all…'

The contradictory replies emerged in unison.

Gabriel met Alice's hot warning glare with a benign good humour that made her teeth ache with frustration.

'Sophie said you were concerned about little William, Alice, so I thought I'd come myself to reassure you he's absolutely none the worse for his experience and fast asleep, bless him.' Her face had a soft besotted expression as she spoke of her newly discovered grandson. 'I've also done the rounds and got a selection of likely clothes.' She placed a large bundle of outfits on the bed. 'Hopefully there might be something amongst this little lot to suit.'

Alice, overwhelmed by this kindness, made some inarticulate sound in response.

'We'll have a nice little chat later on, my dear. Gabe has told us such a lot about you.' *He had?* Alice's shocked eyes automatically swivelled to his. 'I feel as if I know you already. Don't glare at me like that,' she told her son, 'I'm not staying.' She patted his arm. 'You should take a nice warm shower. My reluctant hero,' she added with a twinkle.

'Mother…' Gabriel warned.

'All right, all right,' she conceded. 'Though why you should be so paranoid about anyone finding out you saved Rosanna's life is beyond me!'

Gabriel closed his eyes. 'I just happened to be there,' he ground out grimly.

'And you just *happened* to keep her alive by mouth-to-mouth when the water closed over her head until Fabrizio fetched the emergency services to free her. No wonder the girl looks at you as though you're the second coming!'

Alice stared in shocked comprehension at Gabriel, who had looked acutely uncomfortable during his mother's disclosures. Everything slipped into place now. Gabriel's guilty secret was an act of heroism! He'd not been trying to hide the fact he'd seduced the girl, just the fact he'd saved her life!

'Haven't you got things to do, Mother?' Gabriel enquired hopefully. 'Guests arriving and so forth…' he added meaningfully from between clenched teeth.

'I'll see you both later. Not too much later, Gabriel. You mustn't be greedy and keep Alice to yourself.'

Arms folded across his chest, he watched her leave the room with an expression of frustration. 'There's not much chance of that, is there? When my family treat my room like a public thoroughfare!'

Alice didn't think this was the time to point out that this wasn't actually his room. Head spinning, she sat down with a bump on the bed, her eyes fixed on the tall rangy figure who was shiftily avoiding her eyes.

'You're a hero!' she accused reproachfully.

'Nothing of the sort!' he responded swiftly, with a horror-struck expression. 'That's exactly the sort of nonsense

I wanted to avoid! I was just in the right place—or rather,' he corrected himself drily, 'we—Rosanna, her brother Fabrizio and I—were in the *wrong* place at the *wrong* time. A dry riverbed,' he explained with obvious reluctance, in response to her enquiring expression. 'Freak weather conditions higher up in the mountains meant dry riverbed one second, raging torrent the next.

'Fabrizio and I got out in time,' he recalled, 'but Rosanna was trapped with her leg jammed under a heavy branch. When we couldn't budge it Fabrizio went for help; it made sense—he knew the area better than me. The river rose fairly dramatically, but fortunately the emergency services arrived in time,' he told her, not dwelling on the nightmare moment when the young girl's head had become submerged under the swirling water.

'*Unfortunately* they were accompanied by a camera crew—you know the sort of thing,' he told her sourly. 'Human interest stories in the middle of a disaster.' His lips curled in distaste. And to make matters worse,' he added indignantly, 'Rosanna gave this gushing report from her hospital bed. She made me sound like a…a…' Words failed him. 'It was grim!' he confided with shudder.

Once she'd stopped dwelling on the vivid image of his body lying face-down in a cold watery grave—because she was positive he'd played down the danger of the situation—her chest swelled with a sudden overwhelming outpouring of love for this perverse man she needed more than life itself.

'You didn't enjoy being a celebrity, Gabriel?' she taunted, with wide innocent eyes.

He made a low growling sound of disgust in his throat. 'I was not a…'

'You just happened to be there.'

'Right.' There was a rueful flicker of wry humour in his

eyes as he impatiently raked his hand over the thick hank of dark hair that had flopped in his eyes. 'If you must know,' he admitted in goaded voice, 'I've never been so embarrassed in my life!'

'Shame you're so photogenic,' she sympathised, not bothering to hide her amusement. At least she could feel amused now. The good part was he wasn't in love with the Italian girl. The bad news was she'd made a prize fool of herself!

'And the video...?' She felt her cheeks grow hot.

'I didn't know Rosanna had brought that. Apparently she enjoyed her five minutes of fame so much she wouldn't be parted from the evidence. The Rossis' home—like a number in the valley—suffered appalling flood damage, and understandingly the poor kid was pretty shook up, which is why I agreed to let Rosanna stay with us until Fabrizio gets back from his seminar in Auckland. He didn't want to contact their parents, who are on a round-the-world cruise which is by way of being a second honeymoon. I only agreed on the strict understanding she didn't mention that damned river rescue.'

'But when she heard about me driving your car into the river...' Now his ironic remarks made sense.

'She flipped. Once Greg had left to pick us up she spilled the lot!'

Alice groaned and buried her face in her hands. 'I must have sounded like a...' With an angry sniff she lifted her head. 'Well, I'm not going to grovel! What was I supposed to think?' she demanded. 'With her plastered all over you. You knew I was jealous!' she accused, recalling all the opportunities he'd had to put her straight and hadn't.

'A deep shade of green,' he agreed cheerfully. 'The thought did keep me going—nothing else seemed to be going the way I'd planned,' he confessed. His grin was unapologetically smug.

Alice suddenly felt breathless. 'And what,' she enquired huskily, casting a wary look at him through the sweep of her lashes, 'did you plan?'

'I was planning on going straight to hell.'

'Via Tuscany.' The way he was looking at her made the butterfly tremors in her belly turn into a major hot implosion.

'I changed my plans.' His dark eyes continued to rove hungrily over her face.

'When?' she whispered faintly.

'When I spoke to you on the phone you sounded as though you'd missed me.'

'Will missed you…' Her voice faded away under the reproachful glitter in his eyes.

'It raised the possibility you didn't hate me after all…'

'I don't hate you. I never did, Gabriel. I tried to explain why I…'

He walked over to the bed, dropped down on his knees beside her and pressed a finger firmly to her lips. 'I don't need explanations. We've both done that part. What I need is an up-to-date accurate report on the state of your feelings for me. A detailed report,' he warned her sternly, taking his finger slowly away.

No matter how hard she tried she could not break the mesmeric hold of his solemn expectant gaze. 'What can I say…?'

'The truth.'

Could he handle it? she wondered, taking a deep restorative breath. 'I love you. I'm in love with you…sick with love for you…dream about you awake and asleep…' Oh, help! once she'd started it seemed kind of impossible to stop. 'Well, now you know,' she told him with a hint of defiance. 'Is that detailed enough for you? I know you only want to marry because I'm the mother of your child, and I know—'

'You—' even though his tone was soft there was something in his tone that stopped her mid-flow '—know nothing!' The terrifyingly tender smile that she glimpsed in his face just before his lips touched hers could mean only one thing, and it made her light up inside like a Christmas tree.

'Gabriel,' she murmured, several blissful minutes later.

'Uhuh?' He carefully draped one boneless arm around her neck, his fingers running softly along the inner aspect of her upper arm sending delicious shivers all the way down to her curling toes. Her own quivering fingertips automatically moved over the hard satiny skin of his shoulderblades.

'I don't understand…'

'You don't have to tell me,' he told her with a long-suffering sigh. 'I've met some dense females in my time.' He rubbed the side of her nose with his thumb. The action was so tender Alice felt her eyes fill with tears. 'Three years ago I woke up to an empty bed, and I started off by despising you, but ended up by despising myself for being unable to forget you. You haunted me, Alice.' His thumb now sought the corner of her mouth and then ran along the soft inner rim of her trembling lower lip. 'You never need to be jealous, my love, because you see, you're my dream,' he told her, with such simplicity, such transparent honesty that she finally realised how foolish her fears had been.

'Most men never get that lucky. Of course I told myself at first that it was sleep deprivation that had made me imagine what I'd felt that night. A man has to rationalise things when he's careless enough to lose his dream.'

'Sleep deprivation…?' she echoed, wonder in her voice.

Was this really happening? Lovingly she rubbed her cheek up against his open palm.

'Yeah.' His voice was muffled as his lips moved with shivering sensuality over the delicate outline of her ear. 'We—the company, that is—had been fighting a hostile takeover bid. I'd not slept in a week. I'd only stopped off at that hotel because I was in danger of falling asleep at the wheel. If I hadn't…' The idea of how fate might have robbed him of this moment made him shake his head soberly. 'I had a celebratory drink or five—I was missing the family victory celebrations,' he reminded her, excusing his excesses with a wry grin. 'Then you walked in,' he recalled hoarsely.

There was an almost unfocused expression in his dark eyes as he rested his forehead against the curve of her shoulder. 'I'd never seen anything in my life so desirable. I'd almost convinced myself you were a hallucination, so when you spoke to me I was shocked, and when you agreed to…'

'Spend the night with you?' she supplied huskily as he lifted his head.

He nodded. 'I stopped thinking completely.'

'Me too,' she confessed.

They looked at one another.

'I love you, Alice. I want to marry you because I love you, not just because Will is my son—not that I'm not over the moon about that. I want us to have lots of babies.'

Alice stared at him wonderingly. She might have to get a bit of clarification on the *lots* later, but now there were more important things to talk and think about.

'You mentioned the marriage part, and the babies. Why didn't you tell me you…' it was still hard to say it '*…love me?*' she managed finally. He'd have saved such a lot of unnecessary pain.

What did it matter? He'd told her now. A beatific smile slowly spread across her face. 'Gosh!' she breathed dreamily.

'If I'd known at the time it would be a selling-point,' he assured her frankly, 'I would have.' He gathered her soft pliant body to him and gave a sigh of pleasure. 'I thought at first…'

'That taking me to bed for a week or even a month would get me out of your system?'

Gabriel groaned self-consciously. 'I didn't really say that, did I?' he appealed.

'It was one amongst many arrogant egotistical things you've said to me,' she confirmed, grinning at his discomfiture.

'Well, anyhow, it only took me about five minutes to realise that neither estimate was going to be nearly long enough!' He took her face in between his hands, his expression tenderly triumphant.

'What's the revised estimate?' she whispered. His expression already had her trembling with lustful desire.

'A lifetime might do it.' Unexpectedly he scooped her up into his strong arms.

'What are you doing, Gabriel?' she asked as he took a step away from the bed.

'A man has his standards. He can't be expected to make love to a woman with leaves in her hair.' To prove his point he twitched a sample from her tangled locks. He laughed as she swatted his chest indignantly.

Standing under the warm spray with Gabriel's hands moving over her slick soapy skin she forgave him for the detour. Her flesh was singing from his ministrations. Deep inside the hunger was growing.

Her neck extended backwards in a graceful arc as he took

hold of the wet hair against her nape and gently but firmly tugged. Through her half-closed eyes she could still see his wet glistening body as the water slid over him. His muscular strength was perfectly counterbalanced by an athletic suppleness that filled her with greedy delight.

'Will you grow your hair for me?' he asked throatily.

His clever lips were applied to the curve of her collarbone and Alice's breath was expelled in a long soundless sigh. At that moment she'd have granted him any request—didn't he realise that?

'That night,' he told her throatily, 'when you leaned over me to kiss my naked body, your hair brushed against me so…so softly…' With a half-muffled moan he suddenly lifted his head directly into the water and open-mouthed let the spray wash over his face.

The water was streaming down his face when he eventually shook his head and looked at her, and there was unambiguous desire flaming hot in his eyes. Her own eyes darkened and glazed over as her craving for him became all-consuming.

Still holding his eyes, she ran the tip of her tongue across her provocatively parted lips before stretching on tiptoe to touch her tongue to the trembling water drop on the end of his nose. His whole body jerked in reaction. 'What did it feel like?' Her voice was a sultry whisper.

'It was like a thousand kisses.'

His erotic admission went straight to her knees. 'I don't think I can stand up, Gabriel…' She couldn't; her limbs felt lax and boneless.

'Sure you can.' One strong arm wrapped itself supportively around her trim waist. Alice closed her eyes and luxuriously slid her open-palmed hands over his chest. 'We can do just about anything we want to together.'

'And can we do *anything* here and now?' If they didn't she might just curl up and die of sheer wanting!

His slow predatory smile was confirmation of her breathless query.

'What…what if anyone comes in, Gabriel?'

'Who cares…?' he growled.

Alice, who had let out a low moan of delight as he sealed their bodies together at hip level, didn't. She wriggled sinuously to reassure him she had no qualms.

She gave a squeal when some time later he carried her wrapped in a towel back into the bedroom. 'Look at the time! What will your mother think?'

The ironic quirk of one dark brow was reply enough. 'But don't worry, she'll be much too tactful to mention it.'

'You're a very selfish man.'

'You've changed your tune awful quick,' he reproached, with a significant glance over his shoulder towards the steamy bathroom.

'You're shameless…lucky for you I happen to like shameless.'

'Has anyone ever told you you have a very wicked laugh?'

'No, that's a first.' And not the only one tonight, she reflected with a satisfied little sigh. 'Now, hurry up and put me down so I can find something to wear. I'm bound to look…'

'Incredibly beautiful.'

Alice decided not to correct this inaccurate statement. Between them they picked a more than presentable outfit that more or less fitted. Gabriel could see no fault in the fact that the beaded top showed way more cleavage than she was happy about, but even she was happy with the long bias-cut black crêpe skirt.

Gabriel left her to raid her sister's cosmetic bag and dry her hair while he went back to his own room to seek out something a little more suitable for the occasion than a towel—after Alice had assured him that a towel wasn't the thing to wear for a man who didn't enjoy the limelight!

It turned out Gabriel had flexible ideas about the limelight. Just before they went into the ballroom he pulled her to one side.

'You don't have any doubts, do you?' he asked urgently.

She was thrown off balance by his abrupt question and the obvious tension emanating from his body.

'Doubts…?' she said uncertainly.

'You've always come out in rash when I've mentioned marriage.' His mobile mouth settled into a grim line as he awaited her response.

'Oh, that.' Lovingly she placed her hand against his cheek. 'That was only when I thought you wanted to be Will's dad, not my husband. You do want to be my husband…?'

Gabriel's reply was comprehensive enough to stifle any lingering doubts on the subject. Her hair, which fell in a silken curtain, around her glowing face, slightly damp at the edges, was slightly ruffled by the time they made their late entrance.

'There you are.' Almost immediately Clare MacAllister came forward, with the tall figure of her husband at her side. He smiled a little shyly at Alice, who suspected her own smile might be a permanent feature for the foreseeable future.

Clare caught hold of Gabriel's dark sleeve. 'Your father's been waiting to make the announcement.'

'Can I have a word first, Dad?'

The two men moved away together.

'I'm so glad you found something suitable. You look really lovely, my dear.'

'Thank you.' Alice blushed, conscious that her eyes had been rather obviously following Gabriel's tall figure across the room.

His mother smiled understandingly and Alice blushed even more fierily.

'Are my mother and father here? I should really go and…'

The noisy tapping on the microphone made her, like every other person in the room, break off what she was saying and look expectantly towards the podium. She glanced across at her sister, who was gripping Greg's hand and looking self-conscious.

'Friends, I think we all know why we're here tonight.' There was a gentle murmur of agreement and several glasses were waved in the young couple's direction.

Alice felt Gabriel's silent presence before his hands came to rest on her shoulders.

'But I think I just might be able to surprise you. People who know me know I'm a careful man with money, therefore it will come as no surprise to many that I've decided to save a few bob by announcing the engagement of *both* my sons tonight.'

The murmur this time was a lot louder.

Alice didn't hear the rest of the speech. She wasn't even aware of all the eyes upon her. The only pair of eyes she was conscious of were those of the man beside her.

'Do you mind?' He leaned down and spoke directly into her ear.

'Would it matter?' she enquired, blinking back the sting of emotional tears in her eyes.

He grinned. 'You can't get rid of me now.'

'Who said I wanted to…?'

'Ally! Ally!' Sophie almost throttled Alice as she enthusiastically hugged her sister. 'This is great! We can have a double wedding next summer!' She clapped her hands. 'Wouldn't that be great? Don't you think that's a great idea, Gabe?'

'No,' he replied firmly, putting an end to her transports of delight.

Sophie's smile faded. 'Why not? You'd like it, wouldn't you, Ally?'

'I've no intention of waiting until next summer to marry your sister.' Gabriel's fingers tightened around hers and his eyes, warm and loving, came to rest on her upturned features.

'You've no idea how long it takes to organise a wedding,' Sophie persisted, with the confident voice of superior experience. 'Invitations, reception, church, flowers, cars—and the dress, of course. When do you think you'll be getting married…next month?' She laughed aloud at her own joke.

Gabriel shook his head without taking his eyes from Alice. 'Next week…tomorrow…?'

Sophie couldn't decide whether he was joking or mad.

'Tomorrow,' Alice dreamily replied, lifting her lips to receive his kiss.

They were both mad, Sophie decided, looking from one to the other. Nice mad, though, she conceded with a reluctant smile. She grabbed her gawking fiancée by the arm and led him firmly away.